A Place to Go on Christmas Eve

With My Best and
warmest wishes

Steven Roberts

Steven Roberts   2018

A Place to Go on Christmas Eve

Copyright © 2014 Steven Roberts
All rights reserved
ISBN ISBN 978-0-9896731-4-3
Cover and Interior Designed by Sandra Van Winkle
Author photo by Alyson Kennedy

WmJoy Press, LLC - wmjoypress@comcast.net

WmJoy Press and the "WJP" logo are trademarks belonging to WmJoy Press, LLC.

PRINTED IN THE UNITED STATES OF AMERICA

A Place to Go on Christmas Eve

Second Edition

Steven Roberts

2014

Other Books By Steven Roberts

Christmas On Deery Street-And Other Seasonal Stories

While Shepherds Watched-Stories of Christmas Miracles and Mysteries

If We Were Any Closer We'd Be One

Preface

This collection of stories is a hybrid. Some of the stories come from previous works. These have been re-edited, some fairly extensively. Some sections have been deleted and new ones added. Those with significant changes have been re-titled. In this regard it's a second edition. However, new stories have been added as well. Since there are new stories and the old stories come from two different works, this volume is more than just a compilation. It is also a new book. I paid particular attention in revising the old stories to maintain the theme of each and especially the theme of their original volume. The same applies to the new stories.

I am fortunate to have the support of many. Nothing in this book would have been possible without Alyson. My graphic artist, sometimes editor, and dear friend, Sandra Van Winkle, designed the cover and turned my drafts into a book. The following people have supported me in a variety of ways; their friendship sustains and enriches my life: John Watson, Nell Alfaro, Rick and Joann Armbrister, Austin Gaines, Steve and Linda Wise, Henry Naff, Harry Hall, and Jim and Nancy Carmon.

I would also like to thank Nancy Bradden, Hans Sowery, Glenn Bourff, Randy Coats, and Lew Toms. Their support made this possible.

A Place to Go on Christmas Eve

Gabriel's Trumpet

My mother was a complete sucker for door-to-door salesmen. It didn't matter what they were selling, if we needed it, or if we could afford it, she bought it. Stuff she bought, some things that defy description and purpose, filled every available space in the house. In every closet, in the attic, in the basement, and under every bed were small appliances, kitchen utensils, countless magazines, beauty aids, and any manner of odd looking stuff. Most of them were never used and eventually found their way to their final resting place, wherever that was.

My kid brother Timmy and I became the source of ridicule from the neighborhood kids because of our mother's inability to say no to salesmen. She desperately wanted us to play the piano but any instrument would do. It was a sign of class, culture, and refinement. At least that's what she thought. But learning the piano was out of the question; we simply couldn't afford one, not even an old, used one. Just when she had finally resigned herself that her sons would be just two more of the unwashed and uncultured masses, Lawrence Gilliland rang the doorbell.

Lawrence Gilliland sold musical instruments and music lessons. He was everyone's idea of a bad door-to-door sales-man. He had what my dad called "dunlap's disease"-that is his belly done lapped over his belt. His shirt was always wrinkled and his out-of-style tie reached only to the middle of his stomach. He looked as if he lived in his car and he probably did. The hair just above each ear was combed to the top of his head and apparently lacquered in place. Like two waves crashing into each other, each side curled up and then straight down into a thin mesh of steel wool.

Whether by divine providence or just dumb luck, this was Lawrence Gilliland's lucky day. By the time he made it to our house he had sold every instrument except two. Since my mother had two sons it was a perfect match. Her dream of her house being filled with beautiful music was about to come true.

Timmy and I were three grades apart in school which meant we walked to school together. It also meant he was my shadow. I tolerated him at home because I had to. And when I tried to get rid of him it always ended the same way- his running to mom crying, "Mom, Georgie won't let me play."

Our mother was barely five feet tall and petite in every way. There was nothing and I mean nothing about her that was the slightest bit intimidating or threatening. She was very soft spoken except when Timmy insisted he was being mistreated by his big brother.

"Now Georgie, be nice to your brother. It won't hurt you to let him play with you and your friends."

"Aw mom! Why can't he play with his own friends?"

"Because he doesn't have any friends his own age."

"That's because he's so weird nobody likes him."

"Georgie, he can't help being unique."

"Unique? He's not unique. He's weird."

These little exchanges always ended with my mother's coup de gras: "Just wait 'till your father gets home, young man!"

Our father was also small but what he liked to call "wiry." We never really knew exactly what wiry meant; we just knew it probably wasn't in our favor to find out. He had strong arms and hands from years of loading and unloading freight cars for the Southern Railroad. Like our mother, he was neither intimidating nor threatening. But he had a paddle.

This paddle was no ordinary bolo paddle. No, this was a medieval weapon of torture. It was made from petrified mahogany that was as hard as granite. It was covered with tiny metal barbs that could easily turn your backside into hamburger. Then there was the large spike in the end. At least that what we imagined. It even had a name-Brutus, which provided a very creative topic for a high school English paper.

He had never actually used Brutus. He did point it at Timmy and me once which was all we needed. It was like kinetic energy, always ready to use. It was hidden someplace-we never knew and never looked. We had only seen it that one time and that was enough. So, the legend of Brutus grew in ferocity each time my father uttered, "I'll get Brutus." I was the only person to meet Brutus face-to-face.

Early one Saturday morning, my partner in crime, Fat Wayne, and I decided to re-enact the assault on Iwo Jima in the living room. We placed our infantry legions in the middle of the floor for a full frontal assault. They were supported by tanks and artillery from the rear. Fat Wayne was the Japs and had to defend Mount Suribachi which was located on the arm of the couch.

When we played army, we played army. No imaginary crap for us, no sir. We had dart guns and slingshots with which to rain our ordinance on our enemy. However, the early hour of the assault required bombs and bullets with less intensity and explosive shock than that which a daytime battle required. This posed a dilemma. We usually shot marbles from our slingshot. Obviously, not a good idea indoors. And errant darts would not bounce off the wall quietly.

"I guess we could just pretend" I said rather disappointedly.

3

"Are you kidding? We don't pretend! You know that. Was John Wayne pretending when he hit the beach In Sands of Iwo Jima?" Fat Wayne retorted in his usual authoritative manner. His ability to distinguish fact from fiction would be my undoing on many occasions.

"Do you see John Wayne anywhere? If we wake up daddy we're dead! And even John Wayne couldn't save us from Brutus." Fat Wayne had never seen Brutus, only heard about it. But the legend was enough to dissuade him.

"I'm hungry" (an hourly response and hence the name Fat Wayne).

"You know where the kitchen is," I said, knowing he was already on his way. Fat Wayne knew where everything was in everyone's kitchen and had free reign in all.

"I've got it," he said wheeling around with a slice of Galaxy Bread spread with mayonnaise in one hand and a knife with a glob of peanut butter in the other. "We can use dough balls. Think about it. They won't come apart when they hit something, they can't break anything even from the slingshots, and they won't make any noise if they hit the wall. And you have a whole loaf." It was an uncharacteristic stroke of genius. Usually with food in his hand Fat Wayne only thought and spoke in mono-syllabic grunts.

Galaxy Bread had absolutely no nutritional value. The consistency of the dough was such that you could spread anything on it and not tear holes. It probably had a half-life of five hundred years. We loved it. Mom got it because it was cheap and the bread man brought it to the back door. So, as Fat Wayne stuffed his fat little cheeks with his mayonnaise and peanut butter sandwich, we sat at the kitchen table making various projectiles out of Galaxy Bread in preparation for the ensuing battle.

Our house was the typical post World War II, three bedrooms, thousand square foot, G. I. loan financed house. The rooms were small, the bedrooms were just beyond the living room, and the walls were thin.

There was one door separating the living room from the bedrooms. Armed with several hundred Galaxy Bread bombs each, we went to lay siege to the living room island of Iwo Jima.

We each loaded our slingshots and stretched the rubber bands to the max.

"One, two, three" we said in unison and then let fly the initial volley and the battle, complete with sound effects, was on.

Anytime Wayne and I were on opposite sides we were very competitive. I should have remembered that. He was a bad loser and an even worse winner. So, he was either whining about losing or rubbing it in about winning. The Japanese were winning, which greatly intensified the decibel level of the machine guns and explosions. The more of my men he killed the worse he got. My frustration level was increasing exponentially. But I knew if I blew up the flag on top of Mount Suribachi he'd at least shut up for a while.

I hurriedly compacted five dough balls into one for maximum effect. I put my atomic bomb in my slingshot, took aim and let go. The instant I fired, the hallway door opened and there stood my father, right behind Mount Suribachi like Zeus looking down from Olympus.

Thud!

Apparently, oxidation changes the molecular structure of Galaxy Bread. Rather than a pliable, doughy, harmless ball, what I shot was a white rock. It didn't hit my dad but it would have been better if it had. Rather, it hit the wall just beside his head (I blame my frustration for my bad marks-

5

manship). It didn't ricochet off the wall but buried in the plaster sending plaster dust and Galaxy Bread chips everywhere, including on my dad.

As the dust settled on the couch and my father's skivvies all he could see were dough balls and army men covering the living room floor, and me standing there with slingshot in hand. Fat Wayne had vanished. What happened next lives on in the lore of our neighborhood.

Without a word my father disappeared into the hallway. Had I been spared? Was he simply too tired to do anything? I turned to run out the door and join the circus but something grabbed my arm and whirled me around. And as I whirled I caught a glimpse of my dad as he and Brutus started their downswing. Just as Brutus was about to take its first bite out of my butt I flinched.

Thump! Crack! Crash!

Sounds not normally heard in nature came from deep in my throat.

Screams. Sobs. Gasps for air filled the room.

It seems when I flinched I altered Brutus' trajectory just enough so that it missed my cheeks. Brutus hit squarely on my boney hip. Apparently, Brutus hit my hip in the weakest spot of the wood with enough force to split completely in two. The laws of physics then took over and the split-half sailed through the plate glass window with a very loud crash.

I was floundering around on the floor like a fish out of water uttering great heaves of pain. Fat Wayne was cowering under the kitchen table speaking in tongues. My father stood in the middle of the room, his body quivering like Jell-O, alternately looking at me flailing away and at the other half of Brutus in the front yard. In addition to plaster dust and Galaxy Bread chips, he was now covered with slivers of glass that twinkled in kaleidoscopic splendor in the morning sun. He was frozen, completely pale, the remains of the once and mighty Brutus still firmly clinched in his hand.

Enter my mom.

God only knows what it must have sounded like to her. I'm sure she thought her family was being massacred in the living room. As she rushed into the room my father turned, only to be looking down the working end of his twelve gauge shotgun. The one he had instructed her to use in case of a break in.

"You don't have to aim. Just put it to your shoulder, point, and pull the trigger. Shoot first. Ask questions later," were the only instructions she had received. All she saw and heard was her son crumpled on the floor and a figure standing over him who was obviously the source of his agony.

Being the well-trained combat veteran he was my father "hit the deck" just as my mom fired.

Whoom!

Double-ought buckshot whizzed over our heads and sprayed the room, taking out Grandma's antique china on display in the corner cupboard and the photograph of my mother's last family reunion, the only one with all her siblings and both of her parents.

She had never fired any weapon, much less one as big as she. The recoil sent her flying backward against the couch just underneath the hole in the wall created by a wad of Galaxy Bread. And there she sat. Shotgun between her legs, her hair and face sprinkled with plaster dust, dazed. Then it became deathly silent, except for Fat Wayne's whimpers from the kitchen, and remained that way for what seemed to be three or four hours.

By now everyone was beginning to regain their composure. My father and I were waiting for my mother to react, but she just sat there doing and saying nothing. The incident had completely destroyed the living room, family heirlooms, and the only complete picture of her family. And of course there was my crushed hip. Then the most unexpected thing happened.

My mother stood up, put the stock of the shotgun under her arm as if she had carried one all of her life, and took a thorough panoramic survey of her house. *What was she going to do: shoot my dad? Shoot me?* I had no idea and I'm not sure she didn't either.

"You boys are going to have to clean this mess up before you do anything else today," and then she left the room. She never mentioned it again.

"Are you all right?" my father asked as he got to his knees.

"I think so."

"You and Wayne clean this place up." and he left the room to face the music with my mother.

I had wanted to play the trumpet ever since Reverend Lonnie Latimore did the Easter revival at Broadway Baptist Church in 1962. He was a sight: white suite, white shirt, white tie, and a red carnation in his lapel. He preached and played and played and preached. I wasn't the least bit interested in his sermon. But when the good reverend put his golden trumpet to his lips it was like Gabriel himself came down from heaven and stood right there in the pulpit. In fact, he billed himself as Gabriel from Galveston.

From that moment I was hooked. I bought every record of Miles Davis, Donald Byrd, Freddie Hubbard, and of course Gabriel from Galveston, I could afford, which was very few. If I was at home I was playing them. It drove everyone crazy, especially Timmy, which was one of the unexpected perks.

It happened on a Thursday, Black Thursday as it became known. It was the day Lawrence Gilliland rang our doorbell. And my mother's dream of having cultured sons was about to come true.

Fat Wayne was waiting on the sidewalk when we got to his house. "A band instrument salesman has been in the neighborhood. Everyone's got a new one."

"Whaddya get?

"A trumpet."

"A trumpet? A trumpet? Whaddya mean you got a trumpet? I want a trumpet. You don't even want to play any instrument."

"Better get home. He's at your house now. Maybe he's got another one."

I set a new land-speed record for the last four blocks home. When I burst through the door there was Lawrence Gilliland on the couch watching our mom sign the contract. I quickly surveyed the living room for anything that looked like it might be a trumpet case. Nothing.

In front of the couch were what looked like two instrument cases. One was a long rectangular case too big to be a trumpet. The other was this huge square looking case, also obviously not a trumpet.

"Boys, this is Mr. Gilliland. He sells musical instruments. And guess what-Santa has come early this year." *Had he ever!*

This can't be happening I thought. *Fat Wayne got my trumpet.*

"Timmy, this is yours," she said pointing to the long one."Open it up."

It was a trombone.

Momma beamed with delight. "Play it, Timmy."

Of course Timmy had no idea what to do. Mr. Gilliland had to help him place the instrument and position the mouthpiece which completely covered his whole mouth.

"Now blow." And with a big gasp Timmy blew as hard as he could and managed a faint, metallic squeak. The mouthpiece, however, was not the only obstacle-there was manipulating the slide. If stood on end the trombone was taller than he was. And his arms were too short to move the slide out of first position. Becoming a trombone virtuoso wasn't looking very good.

Timmy could care less about playing any instrument, but he saw this as a chance to butter-up mom. "I love it, Mom. I'll play for you anytime you want. And when I get rich and famous I'll take you with me all over the world."

"Now you, Georgie. The big one's for you." She was beaming.

Since my instrument was obviously not a trumpet, I wasn't the least bit interested. I had no idea, however, the loathing that would soon exist between me and the contents of the mystery case.

I could hardly pick it up. So, I pushed it to the middle of the floor and positioned the case on its back. Just as I flipped the clasp, both sides flung open revealing my musical future.

There it was, in all its glory and splendor. A Model 2353

Hohnica Keyboard Accordion, complete with thirty-four treble keys, three sets of reeds, and seventy-two bass buttons, the concert grand of accordions.

"Oh, Georgie! Isn't it wonderful. Mr. Gilliland says it's just like having a portable piano you can take everywhere.

IT'S AN ACCORDIAN! Not a portable piano. An accordion, I wanted to yell but didn't.

"Pick it up. Put it on. Play something." She was standing now clapping her dainty hands together in front of her chest. "Oh son, I'm so happy."

I couldn't pick it up much less put it on. With Mr. Gilliland's help I managed to get the straps over my shoulders and stand up. I thought my chest would cave in any second. He stood behind me and together we pulled and pushed the bellows as I pushed the keys. My mother was simply overcome with joy. You'd have thought Van Clyburn was performing in our living room.

"Oh, Georgie, it's just wonderful" was all she could say.

Mr. Gilliland helped me put the accordion back in its case. And in a matter of minutes he was off to celebrate the best day of his career. He had unloaded his musical albatross -the accordion. And I was the proud recipient.

Elmer Pollard, the Minister of Music at our church, quickly heard about the events of Black Thursday. Being the ecclesiastical opportunist he was, he announced the next Sunday morning that he was starting the Pollard Conservatory of Music for all children wishing to learn to play an instrument. *How timely and generous,* I thought.

That was all every mother in our neighborhood had to hear. We were all signed up, for a small weekly fee, of course, for lessons with Mr. Pollard every Tuesday after school. Never mind that he studied vocal music and could barely bang-out a few basic chords on the piano. When I pointed this out to my mother her response was, "Well, he went to music college and he's a minister of God. The Lord will work it out." Her logic is still lost on me.

So, Timmy and I became the first students of the Pollard Conservatory of Music, which was a terrible misnomer, unless a bunch of school kids sitting in the same room blowing and plucking, or in my case squeezing, all at the same time with little or no instruction is a conservatory. But it looked really good on his resume.

Every Tuesday Timmy and I hurried home to get our instruments, load them in our trusty Radio Flyer, and pull our musical future past all of our friends' houses to church. The Fogarty boys became the ridicule of the neighborhood. Every street, every corner had kids waiting to taunt and laugh. Oh, the things we do to please our mothers.

Our weekly lessons at the Pollard Conservatory of Music were rudimentary at best. Mr. Pollard either knew enough or researched enough to show us proper positioning, basic movement, fingering, and instrument care. He was pretty good teaching us to read music, so all wasn't lost. But we were pretty much on our own. I must have played the C and G major scales a million times.

I left every lesson angry, angry at my mom and especially at Fat Wayne. He never touched his trumpet except at lessons and then only barely. It was a sacrilege the way he disrespected my trumpet. My trumpet. He should have been stuck with this stupid accordion that I had to play sitting down because it was too heavy to stand up. To Fat Wayne it was just a horn. That's it. Since we were best friends he let me hold it and finger the valves. When I did, it was like holding the Holy Grail.

Mr. Pollard knew how much I wanted to play the trumpet and took pity on me. I stayed after Tuesday lessons and he showed me what he could. I soaked up every word, every note, every technique. Of course, this extra instruction cost me dearly. Since Timmy had to wait too, there was his fee to keep quiet and Fat Wayne's rental fee. The two took most of what I made carrying the morning paper. What was left went toward song books and my own mouthpiece. Fat Wayne never cleaned his. There was always this brown substance inside the lip of the mouthpiece. No matter what I used to try and clean it-Clorox, steel wool, hydrochloric acid-it never came clean. Since I knew some of the stuff he put in his mouth, oral hygiene and disease prevention demanded my own mouthpiece.

Under the cloak of new-found religious zeal I took every opportunity to stop by the church and practice the trumpet. And the accordion, too, just to make my mom happy. How she loved to hear Timmy and me play. It didn't matter that we could only play scales; we were playing instruments which meant class and culture to her. Being the trustworthy kid I was, Mr. Pollard gave me a key to the music room so I could practice whenever I had time.

Fat Wayne's trumpet and I established an instant rapport. Mastery came quickly. It wasn't just a horn as it was to him; it was part of me, an extension and expression of my soul.

Like most churches the Christmas and Easter cantatas were the highlights of the musical year at Broadway Baptist. Elmer Pollard now had a new means of "packing 'em in" for this year's Christmas program. He had learned early in his career that having kids perform at least doubled the typical attendance. He was sure the sanctuary would be filled to overflowing this year. And who was the guest soloist for this year's program? None other than Gabriel from Galveston himself, Lonnie Latimore.

Our little ensemble consisted of a trumpet (Fat Wayne, not me), a trombone (Timmy), a violin, a snare drum, a tuba, an electric guitar, a piccolo, and the ole Hohnica accordion. We were the only ones who could play the melody to "Silent Night," our contribution to the program which was to occur right before the grand finale. For kids who mostly taught themselves we didn't sound all that bad.

The anticipation of getting to be in the same program with the man who started it all was almost more than I could bear. As soon as I got up each morning I'd mark off the day on my mother's calendar in the kitchen. I thought the performance day would never arrive.

Mr. Pollard got our mothers to provide a reception, punch and cookies mostly, for Mr. Latimore before the program. Refreshments also helped to pack the pews. It meant that I could actually meet Gabriel from Galveston.

"Lonnie, this is Georgie Fogarty. He's quite the budding musician" Mr. Pollard said as Gabriel stuck out his hand.

Georgie? Why did he introduce me as Georgie? I'll never be considered a serious musician if everyone keeps calling me Georgie.

"And what instrument do you play, Georgie?"

Before I could say, "Trumpet, just like you," Mr. Pollard beat me to the punch.

"He plays the accordion"

ACCORDION! ACCORDION! Oh the shame of it. Introduced as an accordion player to Gabriel himself.

"I see. Never liked the accordion much, myself. Too much oomph-pa-pa for me." Then he turned to chat with Wanda Wilson whose red, low-cut mohair sweater, at least two sizes too small, caught his eye.

14

I was crushed. My fate was sealed. I'd grow up and live out my days wearing lederhosen playing in a polka band in some Scandinavian restaurant where the waitresses said "Yah, sure," in a thick accent.

Lonnie had several solos each leading to the big finale-Handel's Trumpet Voluntary and Hallelujah Chorus. But this was not the Lonnie Latimore I was accustomed to hearing. His trills didn't have the crisp triple tongue work he was famous for. Something was wrong. And then it happened. Lonnie quietly snuck out. He was positioned in the baptistery so it was easy for him to leave without being seen. I saw it. Mr. Pollard saw it. Just as Mr. Pollard began to realize his ticket to a much larger church with a much larger and more accomplished choir flushed from his future just as the color had flushed from his face, Lonnie was in the men's room flushing the remains of Wanda Wilson's homemade fruit cake surprise.

Mr. Pollard caught my eye and motioned with his eyebrows for me to find Lonnie. It's impossible to be quiet or discreet when handling an accordion. So, I waited for Eloise Tarwater to begin her aria. She had a big voice with a wide vibrato that whorbled loudly. I knew she'd cover whatever noise I made leaving.

I found Mr. Latimore in the floor of the first stall, his arms around the commode, and his head resting on the seat uttering "Take me now Jesus, take me now." It was clear Gabriel had played his last note of the evening.

I hurried back to the sanctuary to tell Mr. Pollard that there would be no Hallelujah tonight. Then the strangest thing happened, something I didn't understand then or now. As I tried to get Mr. Pollard's attention, I noticed Lonnie's trumpet lying on the floor next to his music stand. Without thinking I picked it up, worked the valves up and down a few times, and then stood there motionless. When the Ensemble finished its last song I put the golden instrument to my lips and as if on cue began the Trumpet Voluntary and then the Hallelujah Chorus.

I was actually pretty good at sight reading but this was way beyond me. I had never seen the music before or even heard it before but it flowed from my lips and fingers as if I had played it a thousand times. It was like I was in some kind of trance. I don't remember thinking or reading the notes. I just played. Every note, every measure was perfect. If I didn't know better I'd have said the trumpet was playing itself. Of course everyone thought it was Lonnie playing. No one knew it was me; no one except my dad, who had slipped out when he saw me sneak out. He saw my whole performance. When I finished I was exhausted and exhilarated, confused and awestruck. I had played both pieces perfectly.

Just as I finished, Mr. Latimore sort of staggered up next to me. He looked terrible and smelled worse, but he was at least standing and not begging for the second coming. He looked as bewildered as I'm sure I did. Then Mr. Pollard called for him to step out to receive his praise from the audience who immediately gave him a standing ovation. He looked at me, shrugged and said "Sorry kid, better luck next time" and began bowing as if he were meeting the Queen of England. We both knew his little secret was safe; no one would ever believe it was me and not him playing. But I would always know and he would always know and that was enough for me. No one seemed to notice that I had been absent from the ensemble, not even mom.

Dad helped me load my monster instrument into the trunk of the car, something he had never helped me with before. All my mother could talk about was how wonderful Lonnie Latimore was.

"Wasn't it just thrilling! It was just thrilling!"

If you knew about Wanda Wilson and her Fruit Cake Surprise you'd be singing a different tune, I thought to myself.

"Georgie, if you could only learn to play your accordion like that."

Now *I* need to throw up.

"That's enough, Erma," my dad said from nowhere.

Although I was excited when Christmas Day arrived it was anti-climactic. I had received my gift at the concert. For those few moments I was as good as Miles Davis and Freddie Hubbard and all the other great trumpeters of our time. Even as great as the Reverend Lonnie Latimore.

The Christmas morning ritual at our house was that my dad played Santa and gave everyone a present. We each took turns opening ours so that everyone could see who got what. As my dad gave me my last present he placed it beside me and then put his hand on my shoulder and gave me a little squeeze. This was completely out of character for him. He was not an affectionate man, certainly not with me and Timmy.

When it was my turn I cautiously unwrapped the gift and revealed an instrument case. I quickly flipped open the clasp. There in my lap right before my eyes was Lonnie Latimore's Amati B flat, Tomoni Kato design trumpet. Mom and I looked perplexed at the trumpet and then at Dad, who just sort of grinned at me. And then I knew that he knew. Not knowing what to say no one said anything.

Later as they were in the kitchen preparing dinner, I overheard them talking.

"Why'd you get him a trumpet when he has an accordion?"

"Erma, the boy wants to play the trumpet."

"How do you know?"

"I just know. Besides, I traded the accordion for the trumpet."

"You did what?"

"That's right. I traded the accordion for the trumpet. He hates the accordion. He only plays it to make you happy. Besides, he can't even stand up with the dumb thing." Then silence fell over the kitchen.

I just sat clutching the trumpet, my trumpet, periodically working the valves up and down. Not until many years later did I learn that my dad had made an agreement with Lonnie after the performance; his silence and the accordion in exchange for the trumpet. Apparently, the phrase "front page scandal" caught Lonnie's attention and sealed the deal.

That evening as we all sat in the living room in the glow of the tree my father said something he had never said before: "Play something, Georgie," as he handed me the trumpet. From that Christmas on until his death, every Christmas night he would say "Play something Georgie." Then as everyone settled in for the night I and my trumpet, that used to be Lonnie Latimore's, brought the celebration and solemnity of the day to a close with a heart-felt and very grateful Hallelujah.

Liveoak

There are a few Christmases that stick out in my memory, ones that are so vivid in their detail and effect that my mind runs through them at the most simple reference to Christmas. There's the Christmas I got my first bicycle, a twenty-six inch red Huffy which was much too high and required a run-and-jump start.

Christmas 1967 was spent at Khe Shan just a short distance below the demilitarized zone in South Vietnam and just a few days before the beginning of the Tet Offensive and the bloodiest year of the war.

The first Christmas after my father's death stands out too with his vacant chair at the head of the table.

There's the Christmas my brother, Everett, and I tied our sister's cat to a paper Mache Santa she made in school and then dropped them down the chimney right after Christmas Eve dinner. Wanting to be sure we attached Santa and Cisco the Cat securely we used a four foot piece of rope. Little did we know that our grandfather had just flipped his Have-A-Tampa Jewel cigar into the fireplace, igniting the cellophane fire on the logs just as Santa and his feline bundle hit bottom. The loud thud that followed caught everyone's attention.

For a few seconds there was an eerie silence, one that inevitably precedes disaster. Then with a loud shriek of Cisco went with one end of the rope around his neck and the other dragging Santa now in flames. Over the ottoman where Aunt Myrtle had propped her feet as she slept in daddy's easy chair, under the dining room table, through the hall, on his way to the kitchen and the back door, and to safety outside he went dragging the blazing ball-o-Santa banging against every object in its path.

Our backdoor had a pet door for Cisco to come and go as he pleased. With a mighty leap and perfect trajectory Cisco sailed through the door and onto the back porch. And a second later, the flaming Santa slammed against the back door and remained there, the flames engulfing the red gingham curtains my grandmother had made as a little girl. Completely dumb-founded by the cylinder of fire that was once my sister's award-winning Santa and not knowing what else to do, my mother and her two sisters, who were busily spreading chocolate icing on the triple layer yellow cake, ran from the kitchen alternately screaming "Oh my God," and "Call the fire department! Somebody call the fire department!"

Now, our back porch was a back porch only in the most fundamental definition. It was in the back of the house and it was a porch. It had no railings and only four steps. It was maybe, maybe three feet wide.

By this time Ev and I had climbed down off of the roof. From all of the screams and cat shrieks we knew something really bad was going on inside. We decided to try and sneak in through the back door. If we could get in undetected we could go down into the basement and say we had been there the whole time cleaning clinkers out of the furnace. We figured any act of unsolicited familial responsibility would work in our favor. As we turned the corner to the back yard we stopped dead in our tracks, greeted by black smoke billowing from around the back door, and Cisco hanging from the porch swinging back and forth, back and forth, floundering like a fish on a hook.

There were all kinds of commotion going on inside-women screaming for help, men cussing and yelling "get some water! Get some water!" Cisco just hung there now, motionless, the noose tight around his neck.

"Let 'im hang," Ev offered with satisfaction.

20

"No, you get him loose and I'll get the Santa."

So, Ev grabbed Cisco and began loosened the rope as I climbed on the porch and pulled what was left of Santa through the pet door. It was hot and smoky and covered in black soot. Just as I jumped off the porch and stood beside my brother the back door opened and out stepped Uncle Frank, a bully and a drunk, who was always in-between jobs, and scared us all to death.

There we stood. Each covered in soot, Ev smiling innocently, holding Cisco by his front paws, and me with the charred remains of our sister's paper Mache Santa.

"We saved Cisco, see" Ev said as Cisco dangled by his paws in front of him.

What happened next remains fuzzy and incomplete in my memory. As Uncle Frank stepped off the porch, Ev dropped Cisco, who ran off never to be seen again. I threw the remains at Uncle Frank and off we went down the alley to seek shelter in Ivan McGill's basement. Where we stayed until we knew Uncle Frank would be passed out.

But as memorable as the Cisco Santa Christmas was, it was the Christmas of 1957 that surpasses them all.

Winona, Mississippi, where I grew up, is like any small town in the South, especially in the Mississippi Delta. The courthouse and surrounding square were the center of town. Most folks still made their living either farming cotton or soy beans or through some other means associated with agriculture. There were two main roads in Winona-US Highway 51 that ran North-South and US Highway 82 that ran East-West. Their confluence was the town square.

My father was a salesman. That's not completely true. To be a salesman implies actually selling something. He didn't. But it wasn't from lack of trying. His resume was extensive- cleaning products, encyclopedias, cars, insurance, sewing machines, and women's shoes. It was not until 1961 that he quite accidentally fell into teaching school and found his call- ing. My mother also had to work in order to make ends meet.

My father was weak and cowardly, that's what I thought. He didn't like sports and read all of the time. He never made any money so I couldn't have cool stuff. The cars we owned were embarrassing and cost more to keep running than a de- cent car would. They were junkers held together by rust and engine gunk, and looked like they'd fall apart any second.

He was soft spoken and allowed others to walk all over him. And I was named after him and called Junior all my life. I hated that. It was not until much later that I came to appreciate, or at least understand, why I was his name sake.

My mom was a waitress at Liveoak, the swankiest res- taurant in Winona. Located in the center of the Square, it boasted the oldest address in town - One Circle Square. The town fathers never realized the metaphysical and theological implications of the geometric juxtaposition of the street name; they just thought it was clever.

Liveoak got its name from the majestic live oak trees that once covered the center of town. Their massive lower limbs seemed to embrace Liveoak as a mother would her child. The upper limbs reached and mingled until they formed a lattice canopy above the house and the slave quarters out back. Many an intrepid explorer attempted to scale the trees' summit only to be rudely reminded of the laws of physics which usually brought a trip to Dr. Hammond Willingham's office. It was as if the top branches were off limits to hu- mans, a sanctuary for innocent creatures who later fell prey to progress and modernization. The floor planks were made from the giant limbs and trunks of the live oaks that once stood where Liveoak does now.

Cleofus Lee Jones was the chief cook at Liveoak. A Jones has been the head cook since the restaurant opened in 1938. He was tall and skinny with long boney fingers and over-sized knuckles. He could cook anything-foreign, gourmet, and especially good ole southern fried. He was a master. And his desserts, especially his White Chocolate Marble Fudge Cake and his banana pudding, were simply religious experiences.

A few nights before Christmas, while we were watching "The Perry Como Christmas Special" momma called.

"Ricky, get the kids and come to the backdoor. It's Cleofus Lee." My dad goes by Richard but she always called him Ricky. "Hurry!" Click.

Clad in our footed, flannel pajamas all six of us imme-diately loaded in the car and headed for Liveoak. When we arrived at the back porch, Cleofus Lee was standing on the porch both arms wrapped in towels from his fingertips to his elbows. Momma was holding one arm and Miss Gertie, one of the other cooks, was holding the other.

"What happened" Daddy asked?

"Mr. Milspah was yelling at Marvalene to stop yapping and get busy cooking. Cleofus Lee was putting fresh shrimp, you know, the big ones we get from Pascagoula, in the deep fryer. Mr. Milsaph pushed Cleofus Lee out of his way and grabbed Marvalene and dragged her out on the porch. You know how Mr. Milspah is. No one thought anything about it. He's all the time yelling at the help especially Marvalene. I just happened through the door with a tray of dirty dished when I saw Cleofus Lee standing in front of the stove. His arms were cooked like giant burned hotdogs-nothing but blistered, black skin. When Mr. Milspah pushed him both arms plunged into the fryer. I can't imagine how that hurt."

Aristocratic, rich, powerful, and a Confederate pedigree, Edgar Davis Milspah was as Southern as they come. His family had originally owned all the land that was now the town square. No matter the enterprise, all their wealth was rooted in Liveoak.

Originally, Liveoak was a hotel that began receiving guests one month before the Southern Railroad began its overnight stop just across the street. Only the Milspahs were privy to that information. Imagine that. And from the first day Winona became a favorite stop for carpetbaggers and others intent on reaping the spoils of war.

The bottom floor was a parlor where gentlemen sat on fine sofas, smoked long cigars, and sipped over-priced Jack Daniels whiskey served by beautiful young hostesses in off-the-shoulder evening gowns with plunging necklines. The women were also available for companionship, for a "fee" of course, should a patron be stricken with unanticipated loneliness. The other three floors were rooms that varied in their appointments. The Fourth Floor was reserved for the most well-to-do. The only difference between Liveoak and a common brothel or salon was the caliber of patron.

The slave quarters were out back in a two story frame building. While not fancy, the house was roomy and well-built. Each room was clean, had a soft bed and bureau, and curtains on the windows. By any slave's standard, living in the "Quarters" was the height of luxury.

The slave children played under the massive arms of the trees that shielded them from the blazing summer sun. They ran and jumped and rolled in the grass protected, safe in their own world that was the live oaks.

After the railroad no longer stopped in Winona, the

tourist trade dwindled quickly to nothing. It's one thing to entertain strangers passing through; it's quite another to entertain just the locals. So, the Milspahs coerced the mayor to lease Liveoak and convert it into the town's courthouse and city hall. No one knew the exact terms of the lease but everyone knew the Milspahs were making a killing off the taxpayers.

The Depression brought an end to the lease. Liveoak stood vacant until Edgar Davis Milspah invested his inheritance in making Liveoak into a restaurant. Regardless of its function or historical marker, Liveoak was the symbol and epitome of southern gentility and hypocrisy.

My dad put Cleofus Lee in the middle of the back seat with me on one side and my sister, Savannah, on the other so we could keep his arms from touching anything. Everett, Chloe, and Grace, my younger siblings, road up front.

You'd have never known he was in what must have been excruciating pain. Not one moan. Not one whimper. Nothing, except to greet each of us by name as he always did.

"Clefus," (when Grace was first learning to talk and couldn't pronounce Cleofus; we all adopted the shorter version). "What did ya do to your arms?"

"I burned 'em, Gracie."

"Does it hurt real bad?"

"It not too bad. I'll be alright."

Savanah and I looked at Clefus and then at each other. We had burned ourselves with matches and hot skillets and knew how that hurt. Those were nothing compared to this. How can he stand it, I'm sure we both thought.

I was sitting next to the window so I could hear the conversation between our parents.

"Better take him to Memphis General. You won't have any trouble there" were my mom's instructions.

"But Jackson's closer" my dad replied.

"Jackson? You want to take Cleofus Lee to Jackson?"

"It's closer and he needs a doctor now."

"You'll have to take him to Madison County General and it isn't as good as Memphis General."

"There's always Womack?"

"Womack? Womack! Think about that, Ricky! You can't take a colored man to Womack." Then she stuck her head in the back window. "Ricky, Jr. and Savanah will take care of you. You hang on, Cleofus Lee." Then she kissed my dad on the lips and was on her way back inside Liveoak. "Memphis! Take him to Memphis" she declared with authority as she walked away.

I tried to watch Clefus without him knowing I was watching as we drove down Broadway toward US 51. I could see my dad watching in the rearview mirror, too. And with every bump, every turn I could see Clefus wince but he never made a sound.

"Where 'we goin?"

"To Memphis to take Cleofus Lee to the hospital."

"But I heard you say Jackson was closer."

26

"It is, but we can't take him there."

"Why not?"

"We just can't. It's complicated."

"If I could drive I know where I'd be going and it sure wouldn't be Memphis!"

"Well you're not driving! I am. You just sit there and be quiet."

Just as I was about to blurt-out that my dad was a coward Celfus interrupted. "Thank you Mr. Ricky for taking me. I know it could get you in a lot of trouble." Then he looked at me. "Your daddy's right. There's nothing but trouble for ya'll in Jackson." I was confused. Why would we be in trouble, I pondered. It had never occurred to me that Clefus being a colored man had some unknown and apparently serious consequences.

I noticed the car had stopped. I looked through the front windshield and saw two road signs staring at us: one pointed to Memphis, the other to Jackson.

I closed my eyes and held my breath; I think Clefus did, too. Then we turned and headed south. South, to the bastion of Jim Crowe and modern slavery. South, where suburbanization clarified segregation. South, where we would all be changed forever.

Like most small towns, medical care in Winona was rudimentary at best. We had one general practitioner, Dr. Hammond Willingham, a gifted Yankee physician who could have practiced in any big city but chose our little town so, as he was fond of saying, he could be a real doctor. As gifted and dedicated as he was, he just didn't have the facilities or equipment to handle anything much beyond routine. For that you had to go elsewhere, usually Sunflower County Hospital. However, really serious illness or injuries required a trip to Memphis or Jackson.

Madison County General's resources were minimal, at best. Its doctors, mostly fresh out of Ole Miss Medical School, were underpaid and over-worked, even by Mississippi standards. It mostly served the incarcerated, the insane, and the indigent. And it was the only hospital that would take black people. The Senator James Womack Medical Center was touted as having the best medical science had to offer. It was as far from Madison County General as it could possibly be.

Named after Mississippi's powerful senior senator, who secured federal funds to build it, the medical center had opened just a year earlier with great pomp and pageantry. It was the centerpiece of Senator Womacks's illustrious career and legacy.

None of us kids had been out of Sunflower County; I'm not sure my parents had either. But it was easy to tell when we were getting close to the "big city"-the lights in the distance got bigger and bigger and brighter and brighter until it seemed like day. We had never seen such tall buildings or so many cars or so many people at one place at one time. Or heard so much noise. Back in Winona everything was closed and quiet. Not in Jackson.

I was troubled. Troubled because Clefus was hurt badly. Troubled that some doctors wouldn't help him. Troubled with this new concept called 'colored people." It never occurred to me that because his skin was a medium brown and mine wasn't that he was inferior. I'd been around Black people all of my life and never gave it a second thought. To me it was no different than our two dogs, Snowball (who was

28

obviously all white and named by my unimaginative sisters) and Rebel (the one I named because he was all grey). Their momma had them under the back porch at Liveoak. I never once thought that Rebel and Snowball were any different. The same applied to people. We all had the same momma and daddy, Adam and Eve, didn't we; some of us simply turned out white and some of us turned out brown just like Rebel and Snowball. And that was that.

"You kids stay here. Lock the doors. Cleofus Lee, I'll be right back" he said, his voice shaking with every word.

My father's timidity was always manifested in his gate, if nowhere else. Tonight was worse. But there was something terribly incongruent. I was watching this sheepish, cowardly little man walk into the emergency room at the Senator James Eastland Medical Center to inquire about medical assistance for a man I had just learned was unworthy of the best medical care. Something was very, very wrong.

"Clefus, how ya doin?" Savanah asked with deep concern.

"It's not so bad," Miss Savanah. I'll be alright,"

"No you won't. Don't know why we came here anyway. He's just a big chicken" I said sarcastically.

"Now Ricky, Jr. You shouldn't talk like that."

"It's true. If they wouldn't give you any help before, he sure won't be able to change their mind."

"Ricky!" Savanah said in disbelief.

"Ricky, Jr. your daddy is a brave man. Nobody else was going to take me anywhere, much less bring me here. Takes a lot of guts to do what he's doing."

"Yeah, well, we'll see."

I really liked Clefus. He was smart and funny. And kind to everyone. He deserved better than my dad. Of course, I had no idea the courage it took for my dad to do what he was doing. I mean I didn't even know Clefus was a colored man. Unfortunately, I was about to learn that lesson very rudely.

The backdoor next to Savanah opened with an "Everybody out of the car. Savanah you and Ricky, Jr. be really careful with Cleofus Lee's arms. You other three wait until I let you out.

"We don't wanna get out. We're sleepy," they chimed in.

"That's too bad." You're going in" he said with unheard of authority.

He led the way. Everett and Chloe held the doors open as Savanah and I carefully carried Clefus' arms trying to keep them from moving. The emergency room was extremely busy. But when everyone saw us, the room became silent. All eyes were on us as we stood in front of the nurses' desk.

I noticed instantly (it was hard not too) that Clefus was the only black man in the emergency room. I was still struggling with this very foreign concept of Clefus being different and inferior.

"I told you before, sir, we don't treat coloreds here. You'll have to take him to Madison General. That's where coloreds go" announced the large, matronly nurse sitting at the desk.

"And I told you, ma'am, that Womack was the only place that can treat his burns."

I couldn't believe my ears. My father, the man who let everyone run all over him; who could always be counted on to shrink in a crisis; who let my mother and his mother always have final say was actually standing up to this woman twice his size.

The woman stood up, put both of her hands on the desk to support her weight, leaned forward, and looked down her nose and over her glasses straight at my dad. I could see him trembling and trying to swallow. *This is it. He's done for*, I thought.

"You better leave, Sir. Now!"

He dropped his head and began to turn. *I knew it. I knew it. I knew he couldn't do it,* I said to myself with great disgust.

"It's okay Mr. Ricky. You tried when no one else would and I appreciate it,"

By now the big blob of a woman had sat back down and didn't notice my father had turned around. Copying the same move she had just made he leaned forward, grabbed the front of her starched, white nurses uniform, and pulled her within inches of his face. Surprise and fear quickly rushed over her. Me too.

In 1957 security was nothing like it is today. If there was a guard, he was nowhere to be found. However, I'm also sure that a guard wouldn't have changed a thing. I simply stood there holding Clefus' arm utterly bewildered at what was transpiring in front of me.

"Now, nurse whatever-your-name is, you're going to treat my friend here," he said as matter-of-factly and emotionless as possible. "And you're going to treat him just like he was the honorable Senator himself." She tried to sit down but his death-grip on her uniform prevented it.

"You kids come here. You see that cabinet over there? Go over there and stand in front of it and when I tell you, you pull everything out in the floor. And when you all finish that I want you to go into every room you can find and do the same thing. And scream and yell while you do it.."

31

We all shook our heads, completely afraid not to do as we were told.

"Call someone over here and take Cleofus Lee back to be treated. Let me make this clear. I'm not going to let go until I know Cleofus Lee is being taken care of. And if you don't, this place will look like an A-bomb went off in it. After Cleofus Lee is taken care of, you can call the police if you want to. I won't put up a fuss. But not until then. Do you understand?

"Yes sir."

She called another nurse, who obviously could see everything, gave her instructions to take Clefus to an exam room and have him treated. And to do it quickly without any questions. The other nurse caringly took Clefus and they disappeared through the big, wooden, double doors that led to where the magic of modern medicine was performed. We manned our posts and watched as our father and the nurse remained leaning on the desk, his hand firmly gripping her uniform, their noses inches apart.

"May I sit down? My legs are hurting."

"You weren't even going to look at my friend. Why should I care about your legs?"

Big tears began streaming down her face as she trembled uncontrollably.

"If I let you sit down I want your word that you'll sit quietly until the doctor is finished with my friend."

She nodded.

Then he let go. And they both sat down, she at her desk, he in the first row of waiting room chairs. Then he called us all to him. While I was disappointed not to have reaped havoc in the ER at Womack Medical Center, I was more astonished at my father than anything. Here was a man who had never stood up to anyone; who was bossed around by everyone, especially my mother; and who had never questioned much less defied authority. And he had just done something much greater men had been unable to do; he had just broken the color barrier at the Senator James Womack Medical Center in Jackson, Mississippi.

After a while Clefus appeared with one orderly at each arm.

"His bandages will need to be changed regularly," the young doctor said as he handed my dad a bottle of pain pills. "I'm sure you can get that done at Sunflower General. If anyone gives you any trouble, let me know. The head resident and I went to Ole Miss together. And Cleofus Lee, I'll be glad to see you any time."

Then the doctor looked at my dad. "He needs someone to take of him for a few days. The pain pills are pretty strong."

"I am going to jail?"

"No, you're not going to jail. Frankly, it's about time someone stood up to that cow. Would you really have turned your kids loose like that?

Silence.

"Thank you, doctor, for all your help. Come on kids. Let's get Cleofus Lee home."

Then we all loaded in the car and headed home to a future we could not possibly imagine.

The drive back to Winona was quiet save the almost hypnotic droning of our tires griping the tar-and gravel-surface of US 51. Clefus leaned his head against the back of the seat resting his arms on pillows provided by the orderly and slept most of the way. So did everyone else except me and my father.

I was more confused than ever. I was still wrestling with the "colored man" concept and all that it apparently meant. But now, on top of that, was my dad's behavior. What I witnessed in the hospital was completely foreign, like he had been possessed by an invisible alien or had some kind of out of body experience. I don't know what it was but it was something other-worldly.

My mind jumped back and forth between the two until I became dizzy and gave up trying to grasp all that had happened. What was important was that my dad stood up for Clefus and he got help. And I was proud of him for the first time.

Momma was sitting on the back porch at Liveoak, a Camel cigarette between her fingers and a pile of butts around her feet, when we pulled into the back parking lot.

"You kids stay here. I'm gonna tell Momma about Cleofus Lee." He had never been a match for my mom. *I wonder how this will go, I thought to myself.*

Being the demonstrative woman she was, momma was very animated in her arm and hand movements. She was one of those who might as well be mute if she couldn't use her hands while she talked. My dad just stood there with his hands in his pockets taking whatever she was saying and I had a pretty good idea what that was.

Just as I began thinking, *well, that didn't take very long,* my dad grabbed my mother's arms, held them still until she stopped talking (not an easy thing to accomplish), said something to her, took her hand and began walking her toward the car. *What in the world is going on? Two times in one*

34

night? Something was very, very wrong.

"Ricky, Jr., you and Savanah help Cleofus Lee scoot over and make room for your mother." We did as we were told; we were almost afraid not too.

"Aren't we going to take Clefus to his house, Everett asked?

"We're taking him to our house so we can take care of him. Cleofus Lee, not a word from you. It's already been decided." And that was that.

Clefus stayed with us for over a week. And it was a glorious time for all of us. We waited on him hand and foot which, I'm sure, embarrassed him. I have never met a more gracious and kind person in my life. Like Marvalene and Miss Gertie, he lived in the Quarters; it was one of the perks of working at Liveoak. It had nothing to do with caring about his employees. Old man Milspah did it so they would be on time for work and he could find them if they weren't.

His apartment was meticulous (the Quarters had been converted into three-room apartments years ago), just as I would have expected. I got to go in when we took him home to get clean clothes. It was warm and inviting and I felt right at home the minute I walked in.

On Christmas Eve, the only night Liveoak ever closed early, we all gathered in the living room and listened to Clefus. We were all in our PJs so when story time was over we could run to bed so Santa would hurry and come. First, Clefus recited *The Night Before Christmas*. Then, after a thunderous round of applause, he recited the Christmas Story from the Bible. It was better than watching TV. It was the best Christmas ever.

After Christmas Daddy took Clefus to the doctor regularly. When the news of our little visit to Womack Medical Center and the fact that a black man was staying with us quickly spread throughout Winona, which also made it even harder for my dad to get a job. So, he had plenty of time on his hands. They even made a trip back to Womack just to be sure his arms were healing properly. And when they entered the emergency room, it was filled with as many blacks as whites.

We all paid the price for helping Clefus. We were ostracized by our friends, called terrible names, and pushed around in school. Even Grace and Chloe, who weren't even in school yet, weren't immune. After Clefus went back to his house, he never came back to ours. He was always welcome and he knew it. But he also knew the heavy consequences we had suffered on his behalf. When I left for college, my dad got a job in Memphis and we all left Winona for good.

I had heard something about some black woman in Montgomery, Alabama who wouldn't sit in the back of the bus, and some place in Kansas where black people stood up to white people about where their kids had to go to school. However, it was not until I went to college that I learned what had been going on all over the South, except, of course, in Winona, Mississippi.

After Clefus got well we all fell back into our little routines, and my father reverted to the man he was before. The hard-fought courage my dad had mysteriously found never manifested itself again. It took me years to realize that it simply wasn't his nature and he really couldn't help it. And I stopped blaming him for not being something he wasn't. I never quite forgave myself for not realizing it sooner.

Ever since I became a father, on Christmas Eve I tell the story of how a scared little man and his tall, skinny black friend walked into the Senator James Womack Medical

Center and without fanfare or sitting in the doorway or marching in the streets, helped turn the old South upside down. And I never fail to realize that the greatest gift my father ever gave me was that night, that one very special night, and his one act of grace and dignity and courage at Christmas, 1957.

A Place to Go on Christmas Eve

Full Circle

I was the first of many things in my family: the first to go to college, the first to get a job that didn't require manual labor, the first and only one to leave home. I was also the first to disappointment to my parents, the kind of disappointment that can last a lifetime.

We lived in Blaine, Tennessee, a small, rural community where everyone worked hard, usually farming of some kind; where you didn't have to lock your doors; and where everyone knew everyone.

There are six kids in my family. Ritchie, a brick mason just like our dad, is the oldest. He had no choice about his vocation. He is also a drunk, not an alcoholic, a drunk. Ronnie is a plumber and apparently not a very good one because he is always getting fired. He had been a drunk but is now a recovering alcoholic. The third in line is Rufus who spent all of his twenties in Brushy Mountain Maximum Security Prison for vehicular homicide. Insanely jealous, when he was eighteen he saw his girlfriend in a car with another boy. She tried to explain the boy was her cousin. Rufus didn't buy it. He tracked the guy down, repeatedly rammed the boy's car with our father's pick-up truck, and killed him. Turns out he was her cousin.

The two girls, Althea and Sophia, are next. They are both nurses' aides. Having had lots of practice stitching up their older brothers, it was a natural career choice. They never did anything remotely out of line. I'm the baby. My mother must have been pregnant for most of her young adult life.

My mother tried to get my brothers to enter the ministry. None of them did. Although Althea's and Sophia's gender prevented them from being preachers, at least in Southern

Baptist churches back then, they were still expected to do ministry-type work. I was the one to fulfill my mother's dream. Well, that's how it started out.

My parents named me after Hubert Longmire, the preacher who had been at our church most of their lives. I hated it. My family called me Hubie. I liked Bert. The good reverend told my folks that if they'd name me after him he'd buy them a new baby bed. They did, he didn't. Since she almost died delivering me, momma realized I'd be the last child. I'm sure she thought that naming me as they did would increase the odds of me being a preacher.

I don't know if I actually felt the call or if I really just wanted to please my mother. At the age of twelve, a very appropriate age to begin ministering I thought, I stood up as soon as our little choir started the invitation hymn, marched confidently down the center aisle at the First Pentecostal Baptist Church, and publicly professed I was going to be a minister (preacher was too unsophisticated for me). I hadn't told anyone. My mother beamed. "Oh Hubie, Oh, Hubie, you've made my dream come true," I could hear her say from her regular seat on the third pew. And I had.

From that moment everything I did was directed toward serving God. As far as my parents were concerned, especially my mother, the only way to truly serve the Lord was from the pulpit. I was at church every time the doors were open. I volunteered to pray during Sunday school. I read my Bible several times every day. I regularly visited the sick and the shut-ins. If it had anything to do with spreading the Word, I did it. I studied hard in high school so I could go to college.

I received a full scholarship to Carson-Newman College, a first-rate Baptist school just down the road, which thrilled my mother beyond description. And later, when I graduated from Southern Baptist Theological Seminary, her excitement and pride were immeasurable. During my time at Carson-Newman and Southern I'd fill in for local pastors. I loved the one-on-one ministering. I didn't like preaching much at all. I wasn't sure why.

When I graduated from seminary, based on a recommendation from the Dean, I was immediately "called" to serve at the Peach Grove Baptist Church in Cannons Campground, South Carolina, just outside of Spartanburg. My first Sunday in the pulpit brought my entire family and several of our neighbors to hear me. They filled two pews. I tried not looking at them because every time I did my brother, Ronnie, would pick his nose and act like he was wiping his finger on his shirt.

During the invitation hymn Joey Gordon, who was thirteen and a lot bigger than me, joined the church. My mother was convinced my message brought the boy to the Lord. However, it was prearranged with the former pastor. I never told her otherwise. His baptism would be a sign.

Peach Grove Baptist was like most baptist churches. The pews faced the pulpit platform where the Word was imparted to the congregation. Behind the platform was the choir loft and behind the choir loft was the baptistery, a pool with a glass front where your sins were washed away.

The following Sunday morning, while the congregation was singing the first hymn, I explained to Joey what would happen. He said he understood. "Are you scared?" I asked him.

"Yes sir, a little."

"It'll be fine. Nothing to it." This was my first, too. I was petrified.

When the hymn was over I waddled into the baptistery, my white baptismal robe floating on top of the water around me at first. I stood on a plank that ran from side-to-side under the water. Under my robe I wore hip boots that actually came almost to my arm pits. I read about Jesus being baptized, said

41

a few words about the symbolism of the sacrament, and then motioned for Joey to wade out to join me. He stood on the floor of the baptistery which made the water come up to mid-chest on him.

I placed one hand on the back of his neck, held up my other hand, and said "I baptize you, Joey Gordon, in the name of the Father, the Son, and the Holy Spirit." I had him grip my forearm with both hands and then put my hand over his nose and mouth and began to lower him into the water. Joey failed to tell me he was afraid of water.

Just as the water reached his neck he panicked and began flailing his arms. He grabbed me as if he were drowning. I slipped off the board and down we went. We rolled over and over in the water like alligators with their prey. Arms slapped the water, feet went up in the air, and still we wrestled, splashing water all over the choir who jumped up and ran out of the choir loft.

By this time my boots had filled with water which made it even more difficult to get control of Joey. This went on for several seconds. I thought we'd both drown right there during Holy Baptism. Then with a big, loud groan and a giant push, which created a huge wave that slammed over the glass and reached all the way to the pulpit, I managed to get Joey out of the water and onto the steps where we both gasped for breath.

After a few seconds and realizing the congregation was dumbfounded, I stood up and leaned on the front glass of the Baptistery. Apparently, all of the waves crashing against the glass put too much pressure on the seals at the bottom. Out it popped and what water was left went rushing through the choir loft, across the platform, and into the front of the sanctuary. I looked down at the flooded choir loft and platform and then out at the congregation, who sat stunned not knowing whether to laugh, cry, or fall on the knees and pray.

Not knowing what else to do I raised both arms and simply said, "Amen. Go in peace and God be with you," and sloshed my way out of the baptistery. Joey's baptism cost the church about two thousand dollars to dry and replace some of the carpet. The incident followed me the rest of my life.

The people at Peach Grove were wonderful to me. However, it became abundantly clear very quickly I was not the preacher type. I had a radio show where I would engage guests and callers in theological discussions and moral dilemmas. But the bottom line was I simply hated preaching. So, I daily asked God to make me a better preacher. It also didn't take long for that prayer to be answered.

"Bert, me and Charlie would like to take you to lunch one day this week, if you're available," Bud Anderson asked me one Sunday after the service. Bud was the head of the deacons and his brother, Charlie, was head of the finance committee. The Andersons were not just pillars of the church but of the community-their family founded both. When one of them asked you to do something, you did it.

"Mr. Anderson, it'd be a real pleasure to meet you for lunch." Out of respect for them I never called them by their first names. This luncheon meeting would clarify my uncertain future as a preacher.

As we were having coffee after lunch Bud began, "Bert, I think your talents might lie someplace other than preaching." Then Charlie interrupted. "Son, may I get straight to the point?"

I nodded, caught off guard by their comments.

"Son, the fact is you can't preach. You're great at the personal things, just not delivering the Word." Charlie was a retired Marine Colonel who had served in combat in WWII and Korea. While he was not insensitive, he spoke his mind in a few words.

Bud, ever the diplomat, picked up the conversation. "We really like you, Bert. We think of you as one of our own. How you interact with everyone on a personal basis is better than I've ever seen. When there's a crisis you're at you best. You have a real gift. And smart, don't think I've ever met anyone smarter."

"It's just you can't preach," Charlie interrupted again.

"Alright, Charlie, you've made your point. Don't jump on the boy."

"Mr. Anderson, it's okay," I said to Bud. "You're absolutely right. I've agonized and prayed about it for months." I caught them both by surprise with my candid admission. We all took a deep breath and had some more coffee.

"Bert, do you have any idea of what you might do besides preaching?" Bud inquired.

"I love writing my little messages for the bulletin and I really love interacting with the guests on the radio show. I'd love to study how theology and psychology overlap and the ways that impacts human behavior. I think I'd like to teach college."

"What will it take to become a college professor?" Bud asked with genuine interest.

"I'd love to do it but I don't have the money for living expenses much less to pay tuition. And it would break my mother's heart. To her I'd be leaving the ministry. She'd be devastated."

Charlie looked at Bud then at me. "Don't worry about the money. We'll see to that. We can't help you with your mother." I wasn't sure if they were serious.

"I couldn't let you do that."

"Bert as well thought of as you are in these parts I'm sure we'll have no trouble getting folks to help out. Now, what you need to do is think about it long and hard. And if this is what you truly want to do, then I feel sure it'll happen. When we put our minds to it, we can do some pretty amazing things" Bud said with real conviction.

"How much we talking about, just so we'll know where we stand?" Charlie asked. He could always be counted on to get straight to the point.

"It largely depends on where I'd go. Southern, where I went before, would be about ten thousand, not counting living expenses."

"Is that where would you like to go?" Bud asked.

"I'd love to go to Columbia University in New York. They have a special arrangement with Union Theological Seminary. World renowned theologians, such as Dietrich Bonhoeffer, Raymond Brown, and Paul Tillich, have taught there. I've read all of their books. I could study psychology at Columbia and theology at Union. That would be a dream come true."

"What's the cost?" It was clear why Charlie was chairman of the Finance Committee.

"Counting living expenses, modest living mind you, tuition, books and fees, I'd say it'd take about fifty-to-sixty thousand a year." I waited for one of them to gasp and say, "sorry Bert, there's no way" but neither did.

"Okay, you find out how to apply at Columbia, what it will cost, and we'll get back together," Bud said bringing his coffee cup to his lips as if we were talking about the weather.

"Mr. Anderson..."

"Son, seems to me you haven't quite grasped what's going on here. You're only duty is to get information. That's it. And figure out what to do about your mother. Bud and I have made up our minds. Anything unclear about that?"

"No sir."

"Okay, then. We're all set. We need to get a move on," Charlie said as if he'd just finished briefing his Marine staff. "We'll get together same time next week." And we were done.

As I drove back to the church I couldn't believe what had just happened. The two most important and influential members of Peach Grove Baptist Church had told me I was a terrible preacher, and in the same breath agreed pay my way to two of the most prestigious schools in the country, if not if not in the world. *That's the strangest conversation I believe I've ever had.*

At our next lunch my going to Columbia University and Union Seminary had been irrevocably set in motion. For tax purposes they had established a non-profit foundation, the Anderson Foundation, which to my amazement already had twenty thousand dollars. The Board members were Bud, Charlie, Bud's wife, Judy, their brother, Paul, and their sister, Creole. Bud said that with Judy and Creole on the Board there would never be any question about "where every dime came from or where every dime went."

I had done my assignment and had all the requirements for admission, tuition and fees, deadlines, and anything else that might be remotely associated with attending Columbia and Union. I was visibly moved by their efforts.

"Mr. Anderson, I can't believe people have given money

to help me go back to school. Why would they do that? Outside of Peach Grove no one knows me that well?"

"Bert, you'd be surprised how well known you are. Good work travels fast, not as fast as bad work, mind you, but still fast. While you may not be able to deliver them very well, you have great ideas that have inspired a lot people not just in Cannons Campground but in Spartanburg, too," Bud said.

"You know us and we know everybody," Charlie added bringing the conversation back to its lowest common denominator. "I talked to the Dean of Admissions and explained what a fine young man you are and that you'd make a top-notch professor. After I explained a few other things to her she said she was sure there'd be no problem with your acceptance."

I'd have loved to have heard that conversation I thought.

"In case you hadn't guessed, Charlie can be very persuasive." *No kidding.*

They were both pleased I had gotten all the information and had already completed the application.

"Since both of you hold important positions in the church and community will you write recommendation letters for me?"

"Don't need any," Charlie said matter-of-factly.

"But the application clearly says..."

"Son," was all Charlie needed to say and I shut up.

Bud put his hand on my shoulder. "Bert, don't worry. We've got everything under control. Trust me. It'll be fine." From that point on and for the rest of my life I would never questioned anything either of them said. They were men of their word and that was all I needed. Little did I know how it would manifest itself.

It wasn't but a few weeks until I received my acceptance letter from Columbia University. I immediately called the Andersons. Even though it was a foregone conclusion they were as excited as if I had been one of their children. We agreed to meet for lunch again and plan my departure from Peach Grove.

I announced my resignation to the congregation six weeks before I had to be in New York. This would give me enough time to take care of things at Cannons Campground, find a place to live, and go home and break my mother's heart.

It was time to go before I knew it. Bud and Judy invited me for dinner the night before I left. Of course all of the Andersons were there. As we were sitting at the table chatting after dinner, Bud asked everyone to be quiet.

"Bert, Charlie has a little something for you. But before he gives it to you I want to say something. You have touched all of us more than I could possibly tell you. We all love you. You're a member of our family, and you're always welcome here."

I was about to cry. Judy was-no one had ever seen her cry.

"Son, what I'm about to do gives me great pleasure, more than I thought it would. I'm proud of you," Charlie's voice cracked as he spoke. Then he gave me an envelope. In it was a cashier check for sixty thousand dollars. Sixty thousand dollars. Then I fell apart.

Charlie couldn't talk so Bud took over. "That ought to make a big dent. I know it won't cover everything. Let us know when you need more."

My decision to go Columbia was received as I expected by my mother. I took the cowards way out and delivered the news by phone, something I'm still ashamed of. As my father related to me, "she took to her bed and stayed there for three day and did nothing but cry." When she and I finally spoke my first year at Columbia was almost over. She simply couldn't grasp that there were many ways to minister to people besides preaching. We never talked about it again.

I found a home at Columbia and at Union where my beliefs were challenged. Nothing escaped the toughest intellectual scrutiny. I studied under some of the pre-imminent theologians and scholars and became a disciple of Paul Tillich's brand of existentialism. I regularly found myself thinking *I bet the good folks at Peach Grove and First Pentecostal would think I'm a heretic.* However, not only was I making a name for myself in theological circles, the acclaim and notoriety created in me a much inflated sense of self-importance and arrogance that bordered on total narcissism.

I had distinguished myself so much that upon completing my doctorate I was offered a joint professorship at both schools, a feat unheard of for their graduates. Of course my appointment made me almost unbearable to be around. In a few short years I had written best-sellers, been on all of the TV talk shows, and was paid handsomely to speak at big gatherings. I had become quite the pop-theologian.

I had my own disciples who hung on my every word. Some of my female students regularly invited me for romantic interludes. On a few occasions I accepted, knowing it was against the rules. *I'm too smart to get caught and even if I do they wouldn't dare fire me* I thought. When I did get caught and dismissed from both schools I rationalized *who needs them. I'm a bestselling author known all over the country. I've outgrown them anyway.* Imagine, outgrowing world-class universities.

The years that followed saw me ruin two marriages, make and lose two fortunes, be the center of public embarrassment and humiliation, and follow in my older brothers' footsteps. My addiction wasn't alcohol-it was cocaine, an insidious white powder that seduced me and fed my cosmic ego. When it had me completely in its clutches, it destroyed me and anyone who dared try to help me.

Before I hit bottom and lost everything I had managed not only to repay the Anderson Foundation but also contributed over half a million dollars to do with as Bud and Charlie saw fit. I paid off all family debts. I established college funds for my nieces and nephews, and a living trust for my folks so they could enjoy life in ways they'd never been able to. I even managed to get Rufus out of jail thanks to one of my big-time New York lawyer friends. Ironically, when I really needed money, there was none to be found. My friends all seemed to be in financial straits at the same time. Imagine that.

My fall from grace ended with a very loud thud. I was arrested in a sting operation among the elite of New York's drug addicts. I spent a few nights in jail and twenty eight days in rehab. The latter was a good-will gesture by my publisher before he washed his hands of me, which he should have done long before. He, like everyone else, kept hoping I'd get straight and return to my bestselling form again.

It was the jail time that did it, even though it wasn't but a few days. Watching other addicts puke and wretch their guts out; being surrounded by vicious, desperate people watching me, sizing me up with their gaunt, wrinkled, lifeless faces, probably to do me harm for my clothes and watch, was a mirror of what I'd become. For the first time in years I saw my reflection clearly. And I hated what I saw. They were no different than me except they were at least honest with themselves about what they were. All of us in that cell had betrayed our friends, betrayed our families, and worst of all betrayed ourselves.

There, in that roach infested, urine drenched cell the shame and guilt for what my life and I had become overwhelmed me. I sat in the corner among my many smelly, ragged, end-of-their-rope colleagues and wept bitterly, asking God for forgiveness and grace even though I deserved neither.

Through it all Bud and Charlie and their families never deserted me. They knew about everything-the women, the drugs, everything-and never mentioned it. It was uncanny; no matter where I was they always knew how to reach me. Just at the worst moments one of them would call or send a note. They were always the same: you're always welcome with us, just have faith and things will be alright, we love you, call collect anytime. When I got out of rehab Bud and Charlie were waiting for me. They came all the way from Cannons Campground just to be sure I had a safe place to go. And they were armed with Judy's home cooking.

After they dropped me off Bud hugged me and said, "We all lose our way. Some never find our way back. You're one of the lucky ones."

Charlie handed me an envelope the read "Anderson Foundation" in the corner. "Here son. Whatever you need it for." Then he hugged me, too, and they left. It was the longest time before I was able to open the envelope, which contained ten thousand dollars.

That very afternoon I received a call from the Dean of Brooklyn College. He wanted to see me. He had received a call from the chairman of the Anderson Foundation, "a well-respected organization," he said "that helped others realize their full potential." He suggested that having a bestselling author and noted scholar and theologian on the faculty might be something Brooklyn College would benefit from, especially since the Foundation was willing to endow a chair in the Religious Studies Department. It may have been the potential endowment that cancelled out my infamous behavior. The Dean wasted no time calling.

"They called it the Prodigal Chair. Does that mean anything to you?" he asked with some confusion.

"Yes sir. It does." And in a matter of a few days I was an Associate Professor, with tenure, at Brooklyn College.

My new life and lifestyle were a far cry from my former New York life. My one bedroom apartment in Brooklyn was a little bigger than the bathroom in my previous address on the Upper-Eastside. But I was perfectly happy with my life and myself. I had a new book accepted by my old publisher who was certain it would far surpass the others. It was titled *Sermons I Should Have Heard but Never Did*. Fifty percent of my royalties were to be sent to the Anderson Foundation.

The tires screeched as they hit the runway at Spartanburg International Airport. I hadn't been back in many years. It was a terrible journey from then to now. What I regretted most was hurting innocent by-standers.

Bud was waiting just inside the gate. I hurried to hug him.

"It's good to see you. Where's Charlie?" I don't think I had ever seen them apart.

Bud took me by the shoulders and turned me facing him. "Bert, Charlie's really sick. He has advanced pancreatic cancer. He doesn't have much longer, probably just a few days."

Nothing Bud could have said would have numbed me more.

"I'll tell you about it later. First things first. How are you doing?"

First things First? You want to know about me first?

"I'm doing just fine," was about all I could say.

On the drive into town Bud explained about Charlie. It was discovered about two months ago, that it was inoperable, had spread all over. Charlie was in a lot of pain and stayed sedated most of the time. He was at Bud's house. "Don't let me die in no damn hospital" were his instructions to Bud.

"You want to go by and see him?"

"Not right now. I need to prepare myself." Bud nodded. "Take me by the church, that is if you have time."

"Got all the time we need."

It had been twenty years since I left. A lot had changed. Cannons Campground was hardly distinguishable from Spartanburg. However, there were still several landmarks I recognized. Before I knew it we were at Peach Grove Baptist Church.

"Wow! The church sure has grown." There was a new Family Life Center (the ecumenical term for gym), and a new Sunday school building. The sanctuary was at least three times as big. "Can we get in?" Bud gave me one of those "you gotta be kidding" looks and got out of the car.

The sanctuary was simply gorgeous. Candles and greenery adorned all of the window seals. Red and white poinsettias were everywhere. A huge wreath, covered with white doves, hung just below the baptistery.

"I see the baptistery hasn't changed?"

"Nope. Just as you left it. I can still see you and Joey Gordon splashing around up there, and then you standing there after flooding the whole front of the church and saying "amen." We both burst out laughing.

"Just think, Bert, we wouldn't have any of this if you'd been any good at preaching."

I had basically ignored Christmas for years. I'd send gifts to my family and a card to all of the Anderson's and a few friends but that was about it. But now, back in Cannons Campground, I felt differently. It was like I had come home again, not just to this place but to a state of mind, a place in my heart and my soul that had not be wrecked by cocaine and conceit. It was a feeling of warmth and acceptance. Of unconditional and unfathomable grace.

My purpose for coming was simple: Bud and Charlie asked me to. I was to hold a blessing (Baptist don't christen or baptize babies) for Charlie's first grandchild, a month-old baby girl. I had not come to bury her grandfather who had been a constant source of support. But I knew it was also the reason I was here.

"You ready to go?" Bud asked having come to my motel to take me to see Charlie.

"I don't know if I am or not."

"Trust me, it'll be fine."

We didn't talk much on the way. When we got to Bud's house Charlie was propped up in a hospital bed. This was not the Charlie I knew; he was quite simply a ghost of who he was.

"Mr. Anderson, how you doing?" *How stupid is that-asking a man who could die any minute how he's doing.*

He motioned for me to come closer. Bud explained it took all of his energy to speak. I bent down close to his face.

"Son," *yep, despite his frail frame this was Charlie,* "for a man about to die I'm okay. Will you please call me Charlie?" he said is a whisper.

"Yes sir, Mr. Anderson." We both smiled.

Then Bud pulled out the drawer of the table next to Charlie's bed and took out an envelope. *Not an envelope. Envelopes from them have money in them. They need to be taking care of Charlie and his family, not me* I thought. But there was no money this time. Inside was a hand written note to me. All it said was "Do this for me." The note was clipped to his instructions on what he wanted at his funeral. I was to do the eulogy. At the end of the instructions was another note to me. "Don't preach-you're no good at it." I couldn't help but snicker out loud which pleased him greatly.

He took my hand and pulled me closer again. "Son, trust me. You'll do fine."

"Thank you, Charlie," I said and kissed him on the forehead.

On the way back to my motel Bud told me about when Charlie was first diagnosed. "He didn't flinch. I was the one who went nuts. You know Charlie. He simply asked 'how long?' When the doc told him a couple of months he stood, stuck out his hand and said 'thanks doc for all you've done' and then left. He didn't say anything until we got in the elevator. By this time I'm about to fall apart. All he said was 'Get Bert, he has to do this. He has to bury me.' Then, just like nothing was wrong, we went about our business. Later that day his first grandchild, Ella Josephine (Ella Jo for short), was born and from then on his focus was on her.

The main part of the Christmas Eve service was the blessing of Ella Jo. I had made a few notes on the plane but things were different now. I found myself realizing how many things had come full circle.

The sanctuary was packed. It was filled with the glow and warmth of candles, the smell of fresh greenery, and especially with the anticipation of a special baby. All of the Anderson's were in the front pews with Charlie sitting up in his bed right at the center isle next to Bud and Judy.

The minister went to the pulpit and began by reading the Christmas Story from the Gospel of Luke. He then led everyone in prayer. After the choir finished singing Glory to God from Handel's Messiah I took the pulpit. At that instant, all the events of the past twenty years rushed around me filling me with a new purpose, a new life.

After reading some passages of scripture and some comments on our purpose that night, I asked Ella Jo's parents to join me in front of the Communion Table. I blessed her father, making comparisons to Joseph and Abraham. I blessed her mother making comparisons to Mary, Sara, and Hagar. Then I asked for the baby. After letting her take a few seconds to get used to me holding her I turned to face the congregation.

"Ella Jo, you are a savior. You have come to save us: to save us from the cynicism we create about life; to save us from the despair in our hearts and in our souls; to save us from destroying all that we hold dear; to save us from ourselves.

"Ella Jo, you are a teacher. You have come to teach us the elegance and simplicity of life; to teach us the humility and acceptance of a child; to teach us about faith and trust.

"Ella Jo, you are a messiah. Your linage is not just the House of Anderson but the House of David and the House of Abraham. The blood of three great religions flows through you the same as it flowed through another baby two thousand years ago. You and all others like you are our hope. You are all that we were, all that we are, and all that we hope to become. You are life fulfilled now and always."

With Ella Jo in my arms I walked over to Charlie. I bent down and helped him cradle her, then I put my hand on Charlie's shoulder.

"Ella Jo, you and you Grandfather Charlie are the essence of life-the beginning and end, the end and beginning; the Alpha and the Omega; you are one and the same. Together you have come full circle and will do so over and over and over now and always. You are the filling full and fulfillment of life."

I motioned for Ella Jo's parents to come to Charlie's bed side.

I faced the congregation again and said, "For unto us a child is born; unto us a son is given. And He shall be called Wonderful, Counselor, the Might God, the Everlasting Father, the Prince of Peace. Go in peace and God be with you. Amen."

There was complete silence. No one seemed to know what to do. Then Bud stood and began clapping furiously, and then the whole congregation erupted in a joyous and spontaneous celebration for the lives of Charlie and Ella Jo.

On the way back to my motel Bud asked "When'd you learn to preach" he said with a great big grin.

"Tonight."

"You pick that up at that fancy New York college?"

"No sir. You and Charlie taught me."

As we drove Bud told me their minister was retiring in June and wondered if I could check around for someone good to take his place. I said I still had some minister friends who still claimed me and that I'd be glad to check with them.

"Bud, may I come for breakfast with your family tomorrow? And may I borrow Charlie's car for a few days?"

"Of course to both" he said.

After Christmas breakfast the next morning I asked Bud to walk me out to Charlie's car. Bud handed me the car keys and asked "Where you going, not that it's any of my business?"

"I seem to remember there's place in Blaine, Tennessee that serves a great Christmas dinner. I'll be back in a few days. If Charlie dies before then just call me, and I'll be right here."

As I opened the door to get in I said "And by the way, I'll take the job." Bud just stood there with his mouth open.

"Don't worry, Bud. Trust me. It'll be fine."

The Madam and the Paper Boy

I grew up in a house full of women. My mom and I lived with my grandparents and a variety of her sisters; the number varied depending on who was unemployed or unmarried at the time. My grandparents, Ester and Estes Edwards (I called them Ma and Echie), had five daughters-Buena, Gladys, Annalee, Jocelyn (my mom-Echie called her Betty but no one knew why), and Catherine. All beautiful women, they were a hodge-podge in looks. Buena, the oldest, was a tall, redhead. I never met her but I had seen her picture, one my mother kept in her dresser drawer. Gladys and Annalee were short, dumpy blondes; and my mom and Catherine were short, slim brunettes. Everyone said Buena was Echie's favorite because she was just like him-tough, stubborn, and uncompromising.

We lived in a typical working class neighborhood just beyond downtown. Gentrification had been attempted several times with only minimal success. Most of our neighbors were what Echie called "time card punching, lunchbox totting, working stiffs" who worked hard every day of their lives, except for a two week vacation at Myrtle Beach each summer. They raised their children in the same manner. All of the houses were small, one level with the same basic floor plan.

There was always a running battle between my aunts. Someone was always mad at someone else. Their arguments were loud and punctuated with a lot of door slamming. They yelled at everyone except my grandfather. No one raised their voice to him much less argued with him. Fortunately for my aunts and mom he worked every day and wasn't there much. They never agreed on anything, especially on how to raise me. On that subject they each held very strong opinions.

Every town, at least in the South, has a house that everyone knows about but no one talks about. Our town's was Miss Maybelle Boudreaux's house, a large, three-story colonial at the dead end of Third Avenue. Silent Alley, as it was known, ran behind the house connecting the streets on either side of her house. It wasn't like most alleys; it had one purpose-silent and concealed access to Miss Maybelle's. At one time it was just a path but over the years it became much wider as more and more of her "special friends," as she called them, came to visit. Eventually, one of these special friends, the road superintendent, had the alley paved and promised to keep it in good shape in exchange for her friendship and especially her silence.

The house was on a cul-de-sac and gave the appearance of royalty. In some ways that was true. The grounds were immaculately kept with gardens and beds everywhere. In the spring when the dogwoods, azaleas, and tulips were in bloom is was breath-taking.

Miss Maybelle was a large woman with more chins than you could count. Big fat flaps hung from the underside of her arms and swayed back and forth when she moved. She was always impeccably dressed in the latest fashions. She wore very tasteful jewelry and just the right amount of make-up. She never wore heels. Given her size she still moved with surprising grace and poise, albeit slowly.

She knew the truth about every scandal, every shady deal, every cheating husband, and every alcoholic wife in town. She knew where every skeleton was buried and who buried them. She had special friends in every high position in business and government. And I delivered her morning paper.

For the longest time I thought it was a women's boarding house and, in a way, I suppose it was. I also thought that since laundry was always hanging on the lines out back, mostly sheets, Miss Maybelle's girls took in laundry. I suppose that was true, too.

I, as were all of my friends, was under strict instructions never to go near her house, except to deliver the paper. The penalty for doing so was unspeakable pain and torture. I was never told why. But my friend Johnny Walker had the straight scoop from his father.

One night Johnny overheard his mom and dad talking about Miss Maybelle. "It's simply awful what happened to Reverend and Mrs. Barnett. Simply awful. How could a man of God, one who quotes scripture with such passion, give in to the temptations of the flesh like that? And poor Mrs. Barnett. I'm sure she's just sick to death. This will kill her. I bet they'll be gone soon. Something's just gotta be done about that house" his mother lamented.

That's what went into Johnny's little brain to be analyzed by his less than average intelligence. What came out of his mouth to me was "I heard my mom tell my dad that Reverend and Mrs. Barnett are dying. They both have some horrible disease that he got ministering at Miss Maybelle's and then he gave it to his wife."

"What?"

"Something like polio or TB or some other community disease that's real easy to catch. It's so bad that he got it from knocking on the door."

"You're crazy! You can't get sick from knocking on somebody's door."

"Well, my dad said he took his preacher's duty of laying his hands on sinners far too literally, whatever that means. And that it was his uncleanness that made his wife sick."

Now, I didn't know much, but I did know that you can't get sick from knocking on someone's door.

"You better be careful when you collect for the paper"

was Johnny's admonition to me.

I never actually had to go up to the house. There was a mailbox at the edge of Silent Alley and her parking area. A smaller, rectangular box was under the mailbox for the newspaper. She'd put my money in an envelope marked "paperboy" and put it in the same place. So, I never met her, saw any of the girls, or had to worry that Johnny Walker's father might be right. I felt pretty safe.

My paper route gave me a sense of independence and responsibility. Each week my mother made me put 10% of what I made in savings and 10% in the offering plate at church. My grandfather would laugh and smirk when I'd figure out what my earnings were. "Better get used to payroll deductions, boy. It gets worse," he'd say every week.

I never knew my father. He died when I was a baby. No one talked about it much, especially my mom. From what I could gather he and my mom caused a family scandal. Regardless of who I asked about him they'd all say "Ask your mother," who'd respond with "I'll tell you when you're older." However, whatever my mother did couldn't compare to the scandal Aunt Buena caused.

One spring Sunday afternoon Aunt Catherine, my favorite, was sitting on the front porch reading the newspaper. Everyone else was either gone or taking the traditional Sunday nap.

Here's my opportunity I thought.

"Aunt Catherine, will you tell me about what happened to Aunt Buena?"

She dropped the paper below her eyes, puzzled by my question and how to respond.

"Some things need to stay buried."

"Nobody tells me anything! Nobody has told me anything about my father! Nobody has told me about Aunt Buena! All I get is 'wait 'till you're older'. Well, I'm older and still nobody tells me anything!" I said with as much righteous indignation as I could muster.

"You're right. You're absolutely right! I'll make you a deal. I'll tell you about Buena but your mom will have to tell you about your dad. Fair enough?"

"Fair enough."

"Go into my room and get me a pack of cigarettes. Then make sure Poppa is still asleep. And fix me a glass of tea, two sugars, one lemon."

Off I went on little cat feet and returned in record time with Pall Malls and ice tea.

"He's still asleep."

"If Poppa wakes up then the story is over, no questions asked."

"But…"

"No questions."

She lit a Pall Mall, took a big swig of tea, then a big drag on the cigarette.

"Buena ran away from home when she was eighteen because Poppa wouldn't let her date a boy named Slick, who was exactly what you'd expect from a boy named Slick.

"One Saturday night he showed up at the front door. None of us, not even Buena, ever went on a date unless the boy came to the door and came inside. As she ran to the door Poppa intercepted her, grabbed her arm, and asked where she was going."

"'To meet some friends,'" she told him defiantly.

"'One of them that Slick fellow?'"

"By this time we were all in the living room. Poppa released her arm and opened the front door. Buena tried to stop him but couldn't. I noticed he had his other hand in his pocket. He opened the door and was face-to-face with Slick."

"'Buena here?' Slick said oozing with self-confidence."

"'Yes, she's here and she's going to remain here,' Poppa said with no inflection or emotion in his voice. 'She's forbidden to have anything to do with you. Now Slick, I'm asking you to leave.'"

"'I ain't leaving without Buena. Come on Buena, let's go,' Slick yelled into the room."

"No one had notice Poppa had slipped his hand out of his pocket. Just as Slick tried to push him aside Poppa placed his .45 caliber pistol squarely in the middle of Slick's forehead and cocked it. Buena began screaming "'Poppa stop! Oh please Poppa! Don't hurt him! I love him!'"

"Your mother and I were trying to restrain Buena. Annalee, Gladys, and Ma had taken refuge behind the couch, their chins propped on the back.

"I couldn't see Poppa's face but I could see Slick's. His eyes were like saucers and he was white as a ghost. He was desperately trying to be tough but failing badly."

"'Slick, the way I see it is now you're trespassing. I'm simply protecting my family from an uninvited intruder. Get this straight, one of two things is going to happen: you're going to leave right now and never have any contact with Buena again, or your brains are going to be all over the porch,' Poppa said as emotionless as ever."

"'You wouldn't dare!' Slick's quivering voice belied his fear."

"POW! Everything seemed to stand still as the shot rang out. The sound of the spent cartridge bouncing of the porch floor ricocheted everywhere, getting louder with each bounce. Buena gasped and fell to the floor. Your mom and I clutched each other and clinched our eyes tightly. None of us looked at Poppa and Slick for fear of what we'd see."

"'Does that answer your question?' Poppa said just as matter-of-factly."

"I opened one eye and saw Slick shaking in the doorway, a growing wet streak running down the inside of one pant leg. The .45 was again on Slick's forehead. Then I saw the smoke coming up from the hole in the porch between Slick's feet which were now in a puddle. Then in a snap, Slick was gone.

"Poppa turned, gently un-cocked the pistol, unloaded it, and put it back in his pocket. He looked directly at each of us as he passed without saying a word. We all got the message. Your mom and I managed to bring Buena around and assured her she wouldn't be cleaning Slick's brains off the porch.

"As Poppa walked back to the kitchen, no doubt for some of his special medicine that no one could ever find, he stopped and looked down at Buena. In the same tone he used with Slick he said 'Don't see him again, ever. If you do, don't come back,' and walked back to the kitchen just as if nothing had happened."

"Later that night, after everyone recovered, we banded together, for the only time in our lives I think, to help Buena escape and aid her in her soon-to-be life on the lamb with Slick. We took a solemn oath we would never, even if tortured, divulge what we did.

"In the morning Buena was gone. Ma was overcome with fear and grief. She cried for days on end. We were proud we had helped Buena defy Poppa who didn't know she was gone until supper.

"'Where's Buena?' he asked completely emotionless as the night before."

"No one answered. Ma buried her face in her napkin and sobbed."

"'I asked a question,' his voice a few decibels higher."

"Silence. Before he could speak again your mom spoke up."

"'She's run away, Poppa. Left in the middle of the night. Here's her note. Says she loves Slick and is going off with him.' What she didn't tell him was Buena's note also said she'd never come home as long as he was alive. Poppa hadn't looked up or missed a bite as your mom was talking."

"She laid Buena's note in front of him. He paused, stood up, picked up the note without looking at it, walked over to the fireplace, pulled out his lighter and lit the note, and placed it in the fireplace. Then he walked back to the table, picked up Buena's chair, walked to the backdoor, and threw the chair into the alley. We could hear the wood crack and shatter as the chair hit the ground. Just like nothing had happened he returned to the table, sat down, and looked at each of us just as he had the night before."

"'Buena's dead.' Then he finished his supper."

"Everyone knew we were forbidden to mention her name or anything about her. I don't remember ever hearing Buena's name in his presence again. Of course we'd talk about her and try to guess what kind of life she was having. We just knew her life was filled with romance and adventure, and total adoration from Slick.

"She'd send Ma a postcard fairly often, ones you can find in most any drug store. She knew Poppa wouldn't be home when the mail came. Ma hid them in the inside pockets of her winter coat. After a few years the cards stopped. And when they did Buena was gone forever.

I never had to worry about Miss Maybelle not paying. My envelope was in its place every week without fail, except one time. I figured she was out of town and forgot to take care of it before she left. While I needed the money I wasn't about to ask for it. Then when it wasn't there the next week I became worried. I couldn't let her go two weeks without paying-it was simply bad business. So, the next Saturday morning I summoned every ounce of courage I could possibly summon and rode my bike to Miss Maybelle's to collect for the newspaper.

As I peddled I kept thinking *what if Johnny Walker's father was right? What if they did have some dreaded, mysterious disease? What if I could catch it from the door knob? What if someone sees me? Should I stop and get some gloves and a surgical mask?* I was tormented by uncertainty and fear.

As I approached the steps that went to the second floor where the backdoor was I noticed two beautiful, young women hanging laundry on the porch. They both had on white, cotton gowns and were barefoot. I could partially see the silhouette of their young, sleek bodies as the morning sun shone from behind. I tried not to look. *What am I doing? Being two weeks late isn't worth dying for* I thought as I climbed the stairs. When I got to the back porch they were waiting for me.

"You're awful cute," one said as they both walked toward me.

"Thank you, ma'am," was all I could say. My heart was beating so fast I was surprised I could speak at all.

"And sweet and polite, too," the other said as the both reached to take each of my hands.

That was it. Down I went. Out cold.

When I woke up one of the girls was holding a cold cloth on my head while the other was holding my hand. As I looked up all I could see was a mammoth woman who seemed to reach all the way to the ceiling standing over me.

"Who are you, young man? " Miss Maybelle asked.

"Sonny, Sonny Suffrage. I'm the paperboy."

"Girls, help Sonny Suffrage up and sit him on the swing. You all go inside now. One of you bring our new friend a glass of lemonade."

Without hesitation they did as they were told but not before kissing me on the cheeks simultaneously. After just a few sips of the lemonade my head began to clear. Miss Maybelle stood in front of me in her best matronly pose and expression.

"How are you feeling?"

"Much better, thank you ma'am." Realizing where I was, my heart started racing again. "I better get going. I have other houses to collect from."

"Collect from? Is that why you're here, to collect for the newspaper?" She was not happy.

"Yes, ma'am. It's for two weeks."

"Two weeks!"

"Wait here, Sonny Suffrage. I'll be right back!"

She disappeared through the back door. In just a few seconds I heard a very loud "Adele, get down here!" Then in another few seconds I heard feet hurriedly bounding down the stairs. And in another few seconds Miss Maybelle burst through the backdoor pulling a young woman by the arm.

"Adele, this young man is Mr. Sonny Suffrage. He has his own business the same as you and I. *I'm Mr. Suffrage the business man now.* I like how that sounds. He's here to collect for delivering the newspaper. I owe him for two weeks. Could you explain why young Mr. Suffrage hasn't been paid?"

"I simply forgot, Miss Maybelle," Adele said.

"Would you allow one of your clients to forget to pay you? Of course not."

"Do you still have the money?"

"No ma'am."

"Go inside and get your purse so you can pay Mr. Suffrage."

Adele quickly went into the house and almost as quickly returned with her purse.

"Give me the two weeks payment I gave to you to leave in the box. Then give Mr. Suffrage triple what we owe him." Triple? They're giving me triple?

69

Without hesitation she gave Miss Maybelle her money and then turned and handed me my money.

"Now, do you have something to say to Mr. Suffrage?"

"Mr. Suffrage, I apologize for being two weeks late paying for the newspaper. I promise it will never happen again."

"Thank you, ma'am."

"Thank you, Adele" Miss Maybelle said politely. Adele was back inside bounding up the stairs before the door could slam.

'Sonny, I'm sorry about this." *Back to Sonny again.* "I've been out of town. I told Adele to be sure you got paid."

"It's okay, ma'am. And I'm sorry I got so nervous and passed out."

"Why were you so nervous?"

"I've never been to a house like this, you know, where people talk about what..." I began stammering here.

"What goes on here?"

"Yes, ma'am."

"Tell you what. You come back tomorrow after Sunday dinner and I'll tell you what really goes on here."

She reached out her hand. "By the way, I'm Maybelle Boudreaux." As we shook hands I noticed a sparkle in her eyes that wasn't there before. She patted my hand as we walked to the steps.

"Thank you for everything, ma'am."

"Until tomorrow afternoon, then?" It was more of an invitation than a declaration.

"Yes ma'am, I'll be here." I had no idea how I would get there but I wasn't about to tell her no. One word from her about my little fainting episode and my reputation was ruined. I mean, there I was on the back porch of Miss Maybelle's, two beautiful young women eager to assist me, and I passed out. I would never overcome the shame and humiliation. No, I would do as she said.

After Sunday dinner I told my mom I was going to library to work on a project for school. My excuse was sufficiently vague but with just enough detail. Since I was an A student I knew she'd buy it. I went as fast as my legs could work the peddles on my bicycle.

Miss Maybelle was waiting for me as I coasted into her parking lot. Since everyone in her house was up all night and slept most of the day she was just finishing her usual breakfast: a biscuit with honey and a cup of very strong, black coffee; then a Pabst Blue Ribbon beer, a Pall Mall cigarette and more coffee. This was the only time she drank alcohol and she only had one. "Gets my blood flowing" she chuckled. I quickly learned that a lit Pall Mall was always between her fingers, between her lips, or somewhere close by.

She sat in her rocker and motioned for me to sit in the swing. "What did you tell your mother?"

"I lied and said I was going to the library. I hate not telling the truth."

"Here's what I've learned about always telling the truth. "It's a double-edged sword. You better be careful how you swing it."

She lit another cigarette from the one she was smoking. She took a deep, long drag and exhaled a thick, gray-white

71

smoke ring that got bigger and bigger as it floated off the porch. "Tell me what you think happens in my house?"

I was not ready for her question. She was not one to beat around the bush. I felt faint again.

"Sonny, you get paid for providing a service-delivering the newspaper, right? My girls and I provide a service, too. You have customers, we have customers. You try to keep your customers happy and we do too. And sometimes, when we do, we get tipped for it just like I tip you each week." This is starting to make some sense I thought.

"Do you know what the service is we provide?"

I swallowed hard. "Sex." *There, I said it. I hope I don't pass out again.*

"That's true. But sex is the vehicle for many other services we provide to our customers. We also provide understanding, romance, fantasy, compassion, sympathy, warmth, and the security that comes from holding some one really close. Do you understand?"

"No ma'am."

"Every girl here has had a hard life. Most ran away from home or got kicked out. Some end up here because they didn't know what to do or where to go. Some are hiding out from men who hurt them and would again if they could. I give them a place to live that's warm and loving and safe, where they're accepted without question. Everybody knows that Miss Maybelle has powerful friends and you best not mess with her girls. Does that help any?"

"A little."

"Well, you'll understand some day." *Great, more stuff I have to wait to find out.*

72

At that point she began asking questions about me. For the rest of the time I told what few details there were about my meager little life. I have to say, though, I had never met a more gracious and interesting person than Miss Maybelle. We chatted for a couple of hours and then I excused myself, not wanting to bring suspicion on my subterfuge so I could use it again. As I was leaving she asked me if I would come back, that she "so enjoyed" talking with me. I felt the same way.

She walked me to the steps and then said "Sonny, there are three rules for us to be friends. The first rule is under no circumstance are you allowed in my house. Besides getting me in all kinds of trouble it's not right and you have no business in there. The second rule is you never ask about me or my life. The third is you never repeat to anyone anything we talk about. Do I have your word?"

"Yes ma'am." Then we shook hands and I left.

Sunday afternoons became regular visits to Miss Maybelle's. My mom never questioned my regular library visits. "Must be a really big project" she'd say as she kissed me bye and instructed me to be careful. I think she looked forward to my library visits, too. Sunday afternoon was the only time she had to herself. She worked long hours for terrible pay as a secretary.

Listening to Miss Maybelle was real treat. Oh, the stories she could tell. She'd confirm or refute any gossip going around town especially about prominent members of the community. I did learn the truth about Reverend Barnett. It seems that the good reverend was a regular customer making her house his last stop for Thursday night church visitation. Apparently, this went on for some time until one Thursday night the house was disturbed by the sound of metal crashing into metal. Miss Maybelle sent Reverend Barnett out to plead with Mrs. Barnett to stop repeatedly crashing her car into his new Cadillac Sedan the church had bought him. It was all I could do to keep from telling Johnny Walker the truth.

I was always amazed that she knew the things she knew, not just about what happened in town but about everything. I never knew how long her stories would take because of the regular interruptions for more coffee or more cigarettes. Sometimes I got the feeling she didn't want me to leave. One Sunday afternoon I got up the courage to ask about Aunt Buena.

"Do you know about my Aunt Buena? Since you know pretty much everything that's happened in town, I thought you might know what happened to her?" She stared straight ahead.

"Everyone knows about that. She ran off to New Orleans with some good-for-nothing boy. After a while he beat her up, stole all her money, and abandoned her in the French Quarter."

"I wonder why she didn't try to come home."

"She wanted to but was too ashamed and was afraid your grandfather wouldn't let her. He can be a very stubborn man, you know." I really wanted to ask her how she knew all of this.

"Do you know where she is now?

"Yes and that's all I'll say." I wanted to ask her about my father but didn't.

It was two weeks before Christmas. Annalee and Gladys were coming home with their new husbands, Annalee's third and Gladys' fourth. All of the Edwards girls hadn't been home for Christmas in some time. They all had lived other places except me and momma; I don't think she ever lived anywhere except in our house. If she did I didn't know about it. Catherine moved back home a couple of years ago. She had married a much older man who died of lung cancer just two years later. Like Catherine, he smoked several packs of Pall Malls each day. Seems all of the members of my family did, except momma and Ma, who dipped snuff.

Momma had a regular boyfriend who was a very kind and generous man. He was extremely good to all of us. He treated her like a queen. They'd have dinner together on Tuesdays, Thursdays, and Saturdays. He'd pick us up for church on Sunday and take us to dinner afterward that is if Ma hadn't cooked. They obviously loved each other but never married. He was a Catholic turned Baptist and was divorced. I don't know if my mom had ever been married. But they both agreed it was an egregious sin for them to get married. I never understood it. *Surely God was more understanding than that* I thought when I saw them together.

Ma was beside herself with anticipation that all of her girls, except Buena of course, would be home for Christmas this year. She made Echie buy a really big tree, much bigger than we usually had. After supper each evening Momma and I spent time decorating it. This was our time when it was just she and I. Echie would be watching the T. V. Ma would do the dishes and then rock in her room reading her Bible. Catherine would be in her room with the door closed smoking, playing solitaire, and sipping Jack Daniels.

"Momma, may I ask you something?"

"Sure."

"Since everyone else will have a friend for Christmas dinner, may I bring one, too?"

She turned her shoulders and looked at me. I had never invited anyone home before.

"Of course you can. Who is it?"

Remembering what Miss Maybelle had said about the truth I responded, "This girl who lives on my paper route." Technically, it wasn't a lie. I could see me asking my mother to bring the local madam to our house for Christmas dinner. Yeah, that'd go over big.

"What about her family? Won't she be having dinner with them?"

"She's older than me and doesn't have any family." Again not a lie. "I feel really sorry for her. She's really nice to me. Please, may I?"

She immediately assumed I had a crush on this older, mystery woman. But seeing how important it was to me she agreed. The next morning I set a new record that surely would go down in the paperboys' hall of fame for quickest delivery without a complaint so I could get to Miss Maybelle's and ask her.

Since my visit was unscheduled I would have to knock on the door. Through the window I saw her sitting at the kitchen table. She put a note in an envelope, sealed it, and put it in one of six shoe boxes sitting on the table. Then she put the boxes in a shopping bag and disappeared into the house. I decided not to knock. In a few minutes she came out. She bent down and kissed me on the top of my head. She'd never done anything like that before.

"You're early."

"I hurried so I could get here. I have something really important to ask you."

She took a big sip of the awful looking stuff she called coffee and then a big drag from a Pall Mall. "Okay, Sonny Suffrage, what's on your mind?"

76

I took both of her hands and blurted out "Will you have Christmas dinner with me at our house?"

As soon as the words hit her ears, she spit her coffee all over both of us in one, big, loud, choking cough. I wiped my face as she continued to cough. I was sure she'd cough up pieces of her lungs any second. When she finally caught her breath she sat in her rocker and looked dazed. . "Now say that again."

"Will you have Christmas dinner with me at our house? Everyone will be there and they are all bringing someone. And I want to bring you."

"Sonny, I can't do that. It's very sweet of you to ask me but it's simply out of the question."

"Why?"

"Well, it just is."

"Christmas is when you're supposed to be with your family and friends. You'll be lonely and sad and you'll miss your family wherever they are. Well, I'm asking you to be a part of mine." I was getting through to her, I could tell. "Will you at least think about it? It'd mean so much to me. I've never invited anyone home before." *That ought to do it*, I thought.

She alternately gulped coffee and took big drags on her cigarette. "I'll think about it but don't get your hopes up."

I bent down and hugged her neck. "Gotta get home. Promise you'll think hard?" I said as I hurried down the steps. She just nodded as she lit another Pall Mall.

Neither of us brought it up for several days. My mom was pressing me to finalize dinner plans. Then three days before Christmas Miss Maybelle sat me down on the porch swing.

"Sonny, I'll be delighted to be your guest for Christmas dinner. Let me ask you something. Does your family now who I am?"

"They know who Miss Maybelle is and what her house is if that's what you mean?"

"They may not let me stay once they realize who I am. I'm not going to make a scene but I won't be insulted. You need to understand if that happens I'll leave immediately. Okay?"

"Yes ma'am. I understand but it will be fine, you'll see. I'll put a message in the box about what time you need to be there."

"Alright but I'm not going to get there until just before dinner and I'll leave right after."

"Whatever you say," and off I went to tell momma.

I waited anxiously at the front door watching for Miss Maybelle's car. This was going to be the best Christmas ever. Everyone was going to have someone special for dinner.

"Sonny, looks like she's not coming" my mom said as she put her arm around my shoulder and pulled me next to her.

"She'll be here, I know it. Just a few more minutes."

"I'm sorry, son. It's time to sit down."

I moped over to the table. Everyone was seated. I pulled my chair out.

Knock. Knock. Knock.

"It's her!" I said as I ran to the door. There was Miss Maybelle looking more beautiful than ever. She had a shopping bag; I could see several wrapped presents in it. I took her coat. She was nervous, I could tell. Then I took her by the hand.

Only a small part of the living room could be seen from the dining room. Everyone knew my mystery guest was there but no one could see who she was. The table talk quickly diminished into silence. Everyone was looking to see who'd be coming around the corner to join us for Christmas dinner.

As we appeared my mother gasped. Then all the women gasped. Great, it didn't take long for them to figure out who she was I thought. *At least introduce her, dummy.* My mother, my aunts, and grandparents just starred at Miss Maybelle. *Do something Sonny.*

"Everyone this is..." Before I could finish Miss Maybelle stepped toward the table and said "Merry Christmas Ma. Merry Christmas Jocelyn and so on moving from aunt-to-aunt-to-aunt calling each by name. *This is really weird. How's she know them?*

Then she paused and looked straight at Echie.

"Merry Christmas, Poppa." Time froze.

Poppa? Poppa? Did she call him Poppa?

They all pushed their chairs back and rushed to her, each wanting to hold her and touch her trying to erase thirty years of worry and regret and guilt in that one overwhelming instant. I just stood there repeating *Poppa* over and over. They were laughing and crying and kissing and hugging. This went on for several minutes.

"That's enough girls. Sit back down" Echie said with his usual lack of emotion. He hadn't even acknowledged her presence. *What now? I won't let him insult her,* I promised my-

79

self.

Echie got up and walked into the kitchen. I looked at Miss Maybelle. *She had put all of her hate, her anger, and her pride aside only to have her father respond with bitterness and contempt. It took great courage for her to come here and he smashed it just like that* I thought as I got madder and madder. I took her by the hand to walk her to the door.

"You all scoot down" Echie said to Annalee. Miss Maybelle and I turned to see Echie putting a vacant chair next to him where she always sat. "You can seat her, Sonny."

"You all stop your sniffling." I seated Miss Maybelle or Buena or whatever her name is. Then he said "Bow your heads for the blessing." *Blessing? There's never a blessing. Ever.*

"Dear Lord, thank you for bringing Buena home" he said his voice cracking and filled with emotion. "And happy birthday, Jesus. Amen."

I kept repeating to myself *Miss Maybelle is my Aunt Buena. My Aunt Buena owns a whore house.* After the shock eased a little, everyone began bombarding her with typical questions: Where you been? What have you been doing? Are you married? Stuff like that.

"Settle down. Settle down. There'll be plenty of time for that" Echie said like he had done millions of times before. Then everyone began eating and chatting just like nothing out of the ordinary had happened.

When dinner was over everyone went into the living room for coffee and to smoke. Miss Maybelle (since I had never met Aunt Buena I had trouble thinking of her other than Miss Maybelle) said she need to go. Everyone begged her to stay; her sisters were dying to know about the past thirty years.

"No, I really must be going. We can catch up another time. But before I go I have something for each of you." She got the shopping bag and took out the gifts and asked me to give them out.

"I always believed I'd have the chance to give these to you someday but you can't open them until I've gone." As I helped her put on her coat it hit me-*they don't know she's Miss Maybelle. They just know she lives on my paper route.*

When we got to the door she turned, smiled at me, cupped my chin in her hand and simply said "thank you." At that moment we both knew she would never come back again. Then she left.

No sooner had the door closed than Annalee ripped the paper of her gift. There in her hands was one of the boxes I saw on Miss Maybelle's kitchen table; thirty years' worth of letters and cards to each of them right there in their laps.

I went out on the porch just as she pulled away. *There goes my Aunt Buena* I thought. *She can go back to being Miss Maybelle tomorrow, but tonight she's Buena, Ester and Estes Edwards' daughter, my Aunt, and my friend.* When I went back inside everyone was thoroughly engrossed reading their letters, especially Echie.

A Place to Go on Christmas Eve

Arnie

We never knew what world Arnie Allred was in, we just knew he wasn't in ours. Tall, stocky, and strong he was twenty years old, could grow a full beard in a day and a half, and spoke very little. When he did he mostly mumbled to himself. He had a strange look and an even stranger demeanor. He had this psychopath, ax murderer grin all of the time especially when he walked taking his big, clumsy steps. He couldn't carry on even the most basic conversation but it didn't matter because everyone was so afraid no one wanted to talk to him. While he looked like a man he was just a small boy. We met Arnie right after Thanksgiving holidays in Mr. Davenport's seventh grade Geography class.

There we were listening to Mr. Davenport talk about how Russia's horrible winters helped defeat Napoleon and Hitler when Miss Brixie, the principle, called Mr. Davenport outside. After a brief discussion Mr. Davenport came back in leading Arnie by the arm.

"Class, this is Arnold Alred (his name didn't register until it was too late). He'll be joining our class for a while. Please make him welcome."

Arnie slowly surveyed the room with that look of his. His eyes were vacant one minute, piercing the next. We all slumped in our desks hoping he'd miss us. We didn't know who he was and we didn't care. He obviously wasn't a student. *Maybe he's a student teacher. Yeah, that's it. He's a student teacher* I thought. Then as if through instantaneous telepathy we all looked at each other and thought the same thing: we're doomed.

Arnie took his seat at the end of the first row just inside

the door. We were all equally terrified and, at the same time, fascinated by him. He was just so strange, unlike anyone we had ever met. We'd all quickly glance his way then just as quickly look back at Mr. Davenport. I was drawn to him from the start.

I glanced his way and wondered why he looked like that, like he's alive and dead at the same time. Then his eyes caught me and I thought I was going to throw up on my hand colored map of Eastern Europe in 1942.

Rumors quickly spread through the school about the mean, grizzly new kid who'd been in prison since he was twelve. And not reform school either. According to the rumors he'd been in solitary confinement at Brushy Mountain Maximum Security Prison for the last five years. He was in school as part of an experiment to see if the most hardened murderers could actually be put back into society and function in a civilized manner. And he was in our first class every morning. *Well, he's sure not a student teacher.*

"Did you hear about the murderer in school?" queried Billy Wakefield, the leader of our gang?

"I didn't have to hear. He sat three rows over from me in Davenport's class."

"I heard he whacked each of his parents forty times with a hatchet," Billy continued.

"That was Lizzie Borden, you dummy."

"What difference does it make? I heard he killed them both and then smeared their blood all over his face and then drank it."

"You're crazy."

"Well that's what I heard." Thus the legend of Arnie

Alred grew to epic proportions in just a few hours. I had no idea the impact Arnie would have on my life.

One morning before class I was spinning my lucky Silver Eagle silver dollar my grandfather had given me on top of my desk. I caught Arnie out of the corner of my eye. He was coming toward me. I just knew he'd grab me by the hair, drag me into the boy's bathroom, slice me into little pieces, and flush my remains into the sewer.

"Hi Arnie," I squeaked. He just stood there looking at the silver dollar. He made a circle with his finger. I put the dollar on its edge, held it at the top with one finger, and then flicked it with another. His eyes followed every turn with complete fascination. When the coin stopped he'd motion for me to do it again. This went on several more times. I knew it was about time for the bell to ring. When the last spin stopped he reached for the coin.

"No, you can't have it." *I'm dead! He won't even drag me to the bathroom. He'll slice me up right here.* I looked up at him. He looked dejected. I removed my hand from over the dollar. He picked it up, smiled down at me, and went back to his desk. He began spinning the coin as I had done. The first few times it fell on the floor but he managed to do it after about four tries. *A small price to pay for my life* I thought. *Stupid good luck charm didn't work anyway.*

To be cool and tough you had to be in a gang. Our gang was more like a loose-knit association. We liked to think we were tough but we really weren't. We did have a gang-like name though-The Knights.

Like all self-respecting gangs we had membership requirements, officers, initiation procedures, a membership oath, and a hang-out house. Ours was Billy Wakefield's father's utility shed. Mr. Wakefield apparently knew something of the sociological importance of adolescent boys forming peer groups.

Mr. Wakefield turned the shed over to us with the understanding that we would clean it out and keep clean. He even installed a couple of extra electrical outlets so we could have more light than just the one bulb hanging by one wire from the middle of the roof.

It was not a large building but it was large enough to accommodate about a dozen adolescent boys. We were able to acquire a couple of couches, a few chairs, some lamps, and a desk to keep our important stuff in. The gang leader, who we called the Head Knight, was Billy Wakefield solely because of the shed. Billy got to sit behind the desk and act important which he took every opportunity to do. We had regular meetings and talked about things to do which wasn't much. We just wanted to feel tuff.

Our meetings were mostly a chance for us to get together and talk about the things near and dear to our hearts-baseball and girls. Of course we knew absolutely nothing about girls. We did, however, have our sources.

Joe Spooner's brother was in the navy and provided Joe, and thus the rest of us, with all manner of photographs and illustrative diagrams. Doyle McIntyre's brother was eighteen and had gone steady with several girls known in the boys' bathroom for their willingness to assist in male sexual education. By the time we got this kind of information it had gone through several tellings and adaptations and most likely had no basis in fact. Unfortunately, guys like Doyle's brother ruined the reputations of many girls just so they could look studly to their friends.

Our most regular and dependable sources of information were Roger Fini's father's collection of "girly" magazines, and Buddy Alexander's sister's book entitled *You're Becoming a Woman*. Between the two we had some basic and general idea of the female body and the purpose of its unique parts.

As much as we loved to talk about girls and sex there was one subject that superseded all others and required immediate attention-our rival gang, the dreaded Tacoma Street Boys. Like all feuds we had no idea why we hated them and they hated us. We just did. The Tacoma Street Boys were tougher, stronger, and meaner but we were smarter and more clever-a classic clash of brawn versus brains.

Our two neighborhoods were separated by a buffer zone of undeveloped wooded land that ran from the back of our neighborhood to the front of theirs. We called the area the "Weeds." There was an imaginary line that established our respective domains-the top half was ours, the bottom half was theirs. We didn't venture into their side without dire consequences. They didn't come into our side much, although they could have whenever they wanted to. When they did it was usually to use us in preparation for engagements with real gangs.

The Weeds had several huge Red and Pin Oak trees scattered about but it was by no means a thick forest. It was mostly filled with underbrush, Mimosa trees, and various weeds that grew to be much taller than us. We had developed an intricate system of paths and escape routes throughout our sector that required navigational skills and local knowledge to avoid getting hopelessly lost in our little jungle. Legend has it that years ago Mike Kainer's little brother followed him into the Weeds and wasn't seen again for years. When he finally wondered out his family had moved to Canada. We had look out posts in the oak trees, built fortresses held together by Mimosa bark, and secret passages into and out of the forbidden land of the Tacoma Street Boys.

Alfred Alred was their leader. His mother called him Alfie but he preferred Butch. To be a real gang you had to have a guy named Butch. We didn't, which is one of the many reasons we were never taken seriously in the hierarchy of local gangs. The closest we could get to Butch was Buddy and Buddy just didn't have the same street fighter, death row inmate ring to it that Butch had. Butch became their leader-for-life by employing the most basic Machiavellian principle-eliminate the competition by whatever means necessary. We were about to learn that the Boys had just acquired an enforcer, their own Goliath, in the person of Arnie Alred, the rampaging murderer loose in our school. Arnie was Butch's older brother.

Besides Arnie and Butch there were three older Alred boys. Except for Butch they were all close in age. When they were kids they used to put Arnie in the garbage can, put the lid on it, and then beat the sides with baseball bats. Back then garbage cans were fifty-five gallon metal barrels. Apparently, at least according to Butch, the bong, bong, bong that ricocheted and echoed inside the barrel was too much for Arnie, and, as he put it, "made him into a real weirdo." But when the older brothers tried to do the same thing to Butch, Arnie broke one's nose, broke one's arm, and knocked the third's front teeth out. From that moment Butch and Arnie took care of each other.

Butch took his guardianship seriously. There was no doubt he loved Arnie and had his best interest at heart but he was not above using Arnie's strength and mental deficiencies, not to mention Arnie's complete devotion to him, to his advantage.

Christmas, 1963 ended the feud between the Knights and the Tacoma Street Boys. In fact, it was the end of the Knights all together.

Our meager little lives revolved around the Knights. Everything we did had the gang's activities at heart. If we got an extra yard to mow or birthday money it was used, at least in part, to further the interest and reputation of the Knights.

With school out we spent most of our time in the hang-out. Two days before Christmas Buddy Alexander's kid brother, Wally, began banging on the door.

"Open up! Open up! Open...up!"

As we opened the door he fell through the doorway talking a mile-a-minute gasping for breath.

"They've (gasp) invaded (gasp)!"

Billy Wakefield, the Head Knight, took charge. "Who's invaded?"

"They (gasp) have (gasp)!"

"WALLY! WHO'S INVADED?"

"The Tacoma Street Boys!" By this time Wally had caught his breath enough to stop gasping but he was still talking so fast we could barely understand him. But the words *Tacoma Street Boys* made us all pay very close attention.

"Okay, Wally, just calm down and tell us what's going on," Billy declared.

After a few deep breaths Wally made it abundantly clear.

"They've violated the holiday truce and torn up the fort.!"

"How do you know?"

"I saw them, that's how!"

"Are they still there?"

"I think they went back to their side."

We all began asking, "Are you sure? Are you sure?" in rapid-fire succession.

"Okay! Okay! Everybody settle down," Billy asserted. "What matters is what are we going to do about it?" It was not a rhetorical question.

"I told you! Didn't I tell you we need protection? I bet their parents are commies," Albert Steiner interrupted.

"Steiner, you're crazy," I interjected. "They may be mean and they may be nasty but they aren't communists."

"How do you know?"

Steiner was born paranoid. By the third grade he bought into Cold War propaganda that communists had infiltrated government offices, police forces, hospitals, the post office, and local churches. He even believed that fluoridation of the public water supply was a commie plot to make us into mindless zombies. He was certain communist spies had killed President Kennedy just a few weeks earlier. He saw a commie behind every tree. He later became president of the local chapter of the John Birch Society.

He was always saying we needed to protect the hang-out and our stuff, and given our lack of physical prowess we needed a gun to do that. We all thought he was nuts and gave no credence to his warnings of an imminent communist takeover. He regularly asked for a "Tommy Gun" for Christmases but never got one. The closest he came to getting a weapon was a water pistol. We became very uncomfortable, however, when he showed up one day with a Remington .22 caliber rifle, a hand-me-down from his grandfather and the source of great consternation from his parents. He also had plenty of ammunition.

The Tacoma Street Boys violated the two most fundamental, albeit unwritten, laws of inter-gang relations: no
raids on undefended territory and under no circumstances
were truces to be broken unilaterally.

This blatant disregard for honor between gangs demanded a severe and immediate retaliation that sent a clear message: regardless of our lack of muscle the Knights were not to
be trifled with. If the truth were known we had done similar
things many times, we just hadn't destroyed their stuff and
we hadn't been caught in their area. So, we set about plan-
ning Operation Christmas Massacre.

We all gathered at the hang-out about noon on Christmas
Eve to exact our revenge and strike a blow for kids like us
everywhere. As everyone's recited his assignment Steiner sat
with his rifle across his lap methodically moving the bolt back
and forth. Showing clear insight to the severity of the situ-
ation Billy told Steiner he was to guard the hang-out thus
eliminating the risk of anyone getting shot. Convinced we all
knew our parts, and Steiner and his .22 had been neutralized,
off we went to defend the Knights' honor and demonstrate
that brains and ingenuity can defeat brute strength. At least,
that's what we hoped.

Operation Christmas Massacre was simple. Billy Wakefield, through our maze of secret passages, would defiantly
go to Butch's house and challenge the Boys to meet us in
the clearing where both gangs would do battle face-to-face
like real men. Billy delivering the challenge on Butch's front
porch clearly indicated how serious we were. They would be
unable to refuse even if it was Christmas Eve.

The clearing was an open area where we had chopped
down Mimosa trees for the bark to use in various construc-
tion projects. It also had an abundance of staubs. Staubs
were tall, rigid weeds that could easily be pulled out of the
ground. If done properly a clump of mud always remained
on the end which made them great weapons: they could be

thrown with accuracy, they delivered a pretty good wallop, and the mud exploded on impact momentarily blinding the victim.

Knights were positioned all around the clearing armed with mud balls and giant clods, an array of different sized staubs, spears made from Mimosa limbs, and a healthy supply of firecrackers and roman candles. If the battle went badly, we had cherry bombs. It had rained the day before so the mud balls were easy to compact. We had taken crap from the Tacoma Street Boys long enough. This was it, our line drawn in the sand (or the clearing), our ultimate mice or men test.

The clearing sloped slightly from our side down to theirs. Because I had the best arm I was positioned behind a mound at the top of the clearing which gave me a clear field of fire. It also had the main escape ditch behind it. We had all of their escape routes covered from both sides.

We waited anxiously. My heart pounded in my throat. I couldn't swallow. I could barely breathe. Billy was hidden at the bottom of the clearing close to the route we knew they would take. We had two or three man teams positioned at equal increments around the clearing. Each team leader would fire the roman candles and firecrackers as the others let fly whatever ordinance they had. Billy would light a pack of firecrackers when the Boys were all in the clearing both to surprise them and signal to the rest of us to rain mud and fireballs down on our unsuspecting enemies surrounded in the clearing.

Max Goode, the smallest and stealthiest Knight, was the communications runner. He also had an accurate arm. He was to make his way through the undergrowth to pass the word "they're coming." When he reached the mound he was to be on my team. With the Boys dazed and confused by the roman candles and firecrackers we would pick them off one-by-one with our earthen bombs and spears. I had a cardboard periscope I bought at W. T. Grants Department

Store for fifty cents. I always knew it would come in handy someday. That day was now.

When I saw them enter the clearing I froze. Arnie, the ex-convict from my geography class, was leading the way with Butch safely behind him. *We have to call it off. Arnie would kill us all* I thought. But it was too late. The massacre had been irreversibly set in motion.

I could tell they thought this would be like all the other battles-they'd beat us up and we'd turn and run back to the club house bleeding and bruised and secure in the knowl-edge that we were no match for the Tacoma Street Boys. And never would be. *We're all dead! We're all dead!* I kept repeating to myself.

All of the other Boys had formed lines on either side of Arnie and Butch and stood in the middle of the clearing oozing with self confidence in what would surely be yet an-other in a long line of butt-whippings they had inflected on us.

"Come on out you bunch of babies. Let's..."

Rat-a-tat-a-tat-a-tat-a-tat-a-tat.

In a split second Max and I were on top of the mound, arms cocked and ready. Red and green fireballs swooshed from their cardboard tubes and bounced off of the Boys now stunned and bewildered. Staubs rained from the air like ar-rows from Alexander's archers striking the Boys all over. Mud balls whizzed through the air like cannon balls. The Boys were hoping and jumping and screaming grabbing their heads and arms and stomachs not knowing what to do or where to run. Every exit was caught in crisscrossing mud and fire. They could do nothing except move hap-hazard-ously in decreasing concentric circles.

Max and I were waiting for clear shots. Butch and Arnie

were our first objectives. When the smoke cleared enough I took aim. Just as I let loose the staub with the biggest mud clod on the end Butch turned and faced me.

Thud!! It hit Butch right in the middle of his chest. The only sound he made was a whoosh as the air rushed from his lungs as he fell like a rock at Arnie's feet. The force of its impact, and the wet mud, caused the staub to stick to his sweatshirt. There he lay, spread-eagle with the appearance that the staub had gone straight through him.

Arnie bent over to see about Butch. I could see Butch's eyes were open but he wasn't moving. Arnie rose and turned toward me and Max.

Thud! Thud! Thud! Three mud balls in a row. Max's hit him in the neck just below his Adam's apple. My first one hit him on the left ear. The second one did it-right between the eyes. I could see its impact clearly. But I was surprised to see blood trickling down his nose. Little did I know that Max had put rocks inside the mud balls. The story of David and Goliath rushed through my head as Arnie slumped to his knees. When they saw their leader and champion both on the ground the remaining Boys ran through the weeds and briars clearing new paths on the way to safety back on Tacoma Street.

We jumped and yelled and shook empty Roman candle tubes at them and held staubs high above our heads in victorious salute to our cunning and courage. We would become legends in gang lore. Kids would move out of our way in the hall as we passed by. The Christmas Massacre would be told for generations. Our manhood was established.

Just as the rush from our combat victory reached a fevered pitch Arnie rose to one knee and then stood up. He looked down at Butch who was now trying to suck in what air he could, still lying with the staub sticking straight up. *Goliath isn't supposed to get up* I thought to myself.

94

Everything got quiet. Blue-ish white smoke swirled above the clearing as it weaved through the few over-hanging tree limbs. Then Arnie began walking slowly toward Max and me. His look was one I had never seen before, one that made me want to wet my pants. I was frozen. Max collapsed and rolled down into the escape ditch. *I'm about to die* was all I thought.

Butch had managed to catch his breath enough to get to his knees and utter as loudly as he could "Kill 'em, Arnie."

Crack! I felt something fly past my ear. Butch screamed and fell to the ground seeking cover.

Arnie was still coming toward me. I heard a sound I had heard very recently.

"I'll show you, you commie scum."

Crack.

Arnie went down this time. I whirled to my right.

"Steiner!" I yelled as I rushed toward him.

Crack.

I opened my eyes only to find a stranger's face directly above me. Arnie was looking over his shoulder. *I'm in hell. I've died and gone straight to hell. No waiting for the rapture, no purgatory. Nope, straight to hell* I thought very confused. My surroundings were unfamiliar. We were moving but I had no idea how or where.

"How ya doin?" the stranger asked.

"My head hurts and I have this awful pain in my shoulder."

"That's because you've been shot. Clean wound, though. Went straight through. You'll be fine."

"I've been what?"

"What's your name?"

"Danny Cochran."

"Danny, can you tell us what happened?

Of course I can't tell you. I didn't even know I'd been shot.

"No sir. I have no idea."

"You think maybe this gorilla behind me did it?"

"I don't know who did but I do know it wasn't him."

"We thought maybe it was an accident. It's the strangest thing though. He shows up at Fire Station 11 with you in his arms. Blood all over both of you. He's been shot, too. Looks like a bullet grazed his head and another went through his shirt pocket. But we can't touch him. We've tried. Thought he'd break my wrist. All he'd say was 'you fix him, you fix him.' As soon as we started on you he let go."

"What about Butch and the others?"

"Who's Butch? There're no others. Just you and King Kong, here."

"You fix him," Arnie said with some authority just as I passed out.

When I opened my eyes again I was greeted by a beautiful young woman with a white pointy hat and starched white uniform. She was putting a bandage over the hole in my shoulder. Her touch was soft and soothing.

"Welcome back, Danny." Her voice was as smooth as a summer breeze.

I'm in heaven. God felt sorry for me and grabbed me out of hell and took me to heaven with this wonderful angel to look after me I thought as I smiled back at her.

"Where am I?"

"The emergency room. Who's your friend here? I need to check him out, too, but no one can get close enough to take a look at him. He's a scary guy, you know."

Boy, do I ever.

Just then Arnie's face appeared over her shoulder. "You fix him," was all he'd say.

I wasn't sure what to do. Arnie's face had a look I hadn't seen before. It was fear. He was afraid, but of what? No one was going to touch him; he'd made that very clear.

"Danny, we need to call your parents. We have no information on you. And all your friend will say is 'you fix him.'"

I gave the nurse my number and my parents' names. It took some coaxing from me to get Arnie to let the nurse leave the room to call my folks. Apparently, as long as he thought they were tending to me he was fine. However, if he thought they weren't then he became adamant and demonstrated his super human strength and tolerance for pain

"Your folks are on the way. I didn't go into much detail. I said you were in an accident and a friend had brought you here. I assured them you would be alright. Now, what can you tell me about him?" I know she assumed he was an adult.

97

"Ma'am, you need to call his mother, too. His name is Arnie Alred. He lives on Tacoma Street. I don't know the address or his mother's name. His house is about mid-way down the block."

"See if you can get him to let me look at his head and chest while I go try to reach his mother. He's got to be in a lot of pain."

The nurse left the room. I raised my left arm and motioned for Arnie to come closer.

"Arnie, shake my hand." He took my hand and squeezed it but his touch was as gentle as the nurse's. "Arnie, thank you for saving my life. I'll never forget it. Now, I want you to listen to me," I said as if I were talking to a six year old. "When the nurse comes back I want you to let her to fix your head."

"Fix you."

"They've fixed me. I just have to rest for a while. I'll be fine. But they need to fix you now." He looked puzzled. "Now that we're friends we have to take care of each other. And since Butch isn't here I have to take care of you."

His expression instantly changed from concern to almost joy. It was hard to describe. Then he said, "Okay, they fix me."

He remained at my side holding my hand until the nurse returned.

"There's no Alred on Tacoma Street. We have no idea where to go from here."

"That's okay, I'll take care of him. He says you can fix him now. Arnie, this very nice nurse is going to look at the cut on your head. She won't hurt you and then you need to take your jacket off. Okay?"

He nodded slightly and said "fix me now."

The nurse came over to him and attempted to take his hand out of mine. She gave him that same disarming smile as she gave me and he released my hand.

"Will you take off you jacket for me, Arnie?" her voice as soothing as ever. I nodded in agreement and he took it off. "Now Arnie, I need for you to take your shirt off." Even I could see where the bullet had gone through his shirt pocket. Again, he did as was requested. He seemed embarrassed to be naked from the waist up in front of a woman.

"That's funny. There's no wound. Not even a scratch, not a red mark. Nothing. Hmm?" Then the nurse moved her attention to the cut on his head. "This will be fine. It doesn't even require stitches." She cleaned his head and closed it with several butterfly strips. After he put his shirt back on he came over to the bed and took my hand again and simply said "friends."

It wasn't long before my parents showed up. My mother was absolutely beside herself. Of course we hadn't said anything about the Christmas Massacre, and since Arnie had taken me to the fire hall no one knew where I was.

"Oh my baby, my poor baby," she said trying to hug me.

"Ow! That hurts momma."

"Who's this?" she said looking at Arnie.

"He's a friend. He's the one that got me here. It's a long story."

I overheard the nurse telling my dad that I needed to stay overnight. They wanted to give me strong antibiotics and watch me to be sure my wound didn't get infected. I'd be moved to a regular floor in a little while.

"Dad, could you come over here, please?" My father had yet to see my protector. He was taken aback at Arnie's size and apparent age.

"This is Arnie Alred. He lives on Tacoma. I don't know which house (Billy Wakefield was the only member of the Knights who knew where he lived). You need to take him and try and find his mother. Call the Wakefields if you have to. His mom doesn't know where he is either."

"Okay, son. C'mon Arnie. Let's go find your mother." But Arnie wasn't leaving. My dad tried to tug on his arm a little which brought a take-your-hand-off-me-before-I-break-your-arm look. Arnie grasped the rails of the bed so hard I thought he'd break them in two. "Just leave him here and go find his mother," I said.

It wasn't long before an orderly came to take me to my room.

"Whatever you do let Arnie, here, go with us," I told the orderly. "Let him hold onto the rail and we'll all be fine." With that I was on our way to my own hospital room complete with my mother, who had finally stopped saying "my poor baby," and Arnie Allred.

Not long after I got to my room my dad came in. He had no luck finding Arnie's mother. It wouldn't have mattered. Arnie wasn't going anywhere that I wasn't going. "The Wakefields weren't home either," my dad said. I was sure Arnie's family was searching for him and had no idea where he was or that he was safe with me. My dad didn't stay. Someone needed to watch my brothers and sisters, and help Santa. So, my mom stayed.

It wasn't long before my mom fell asleep in the chair.

Arnie stood beside my bed standing guard. The events of Christmas Eve were still fuzzy. I had figured out that Steiner shot me instead of Arnie. *But what about Butch and the rest of them?* I also figured out why he took me to the Fire Hall. It was the only place he knew where people would help me. *He walked over three miles carrying me* I thought in amazement.

I could see the Christmas lights from down town through my window. "Look Arnie, don't the Christmas lights look nice?" He turned to look out the window. When he turned back he took off his jacket and unbuttoned the top shirt. When he got to the second shirt he reached in the pocket and took something out and then put it in my hand. It was my lucky silver dollar with a .22 slug buried right in the middle. "That's why there was no wound" I said out loud. Arnie just kept looking out the window and said nothing.

Not long after we got home Christmas morning Butch knocked on our door. He saw Arnie and ran up and hugged him. I explained what had happened, that Arnie was alright, and that we had tried to find them. Even when Butch tried to take him home he wouldn't go until I said it was alright.

Everyone blamed Arnie for what happened. No matter how hard I tried to explain he wasn't the culprit, no one believed me. And none of us told the truth about the massacre either-it was a matter of honor, the unwritten law.

When they left my house that Christmas morning it was the last time I saw Arnie. The little experiment of putting him in a regular classroom for a certain period of time each day had failed badly. I didn't understand until years later why Arnie was put into our class at all.

He was institutionalized in a state hospital where, as I understand it, he spent the rest of his days. Although I think of him often, each Christmas I get out the silver dollar that probably saved his life and spin it on the table. While it's spinning I say a little prayer: "Thank you for fixing me, Arnie. Thank you for showing true friendship. Thank you for teaching me the transforming power and unconditional grace and love. I love you, Arnie, wherever you are."

A Place to Go on Christmas Eve

Everyone called him Blondie. Most didn't know why. He was born Othello Lafayette Jones. His childhood friends had trouble saying his name. It was long and cumbersome and unusual, especially his first name. Most pronounced it Oh-th-e-lo or Ah-th-a-lo. Ellen Colleen Morarity labeled him Blondie. And he loved to tell how he got his name.

"We used to sit on the huge white marble stones that served as a retaining wall between our yard and the sidewalk. It was a natural sitting wall, especially in the summer when the heavy stones provided the only cool place from the late-July heat. We'd sit on the stones in our underwear for hours at a time. At night we'd tell ghost stories and catch lightning bugs in mayonnaise jars so we could put them on our window seals and let them blink us to sleep.

"One especially hot day I was sitting in my favorite spot on the wall watching a new family move in across the street. I was six at the time. A caravan of beat-up Ford pickup trucks pulled up across the street. They were loaded far above the side rails with chests, appliances, and bed frames. Boxes of kitchen and household items, small tables, and mounds of clothing filled the inside of the truck beds. Each truck had at least one mattress draped across the roof of the cab and tied down from bumper-to-bumper. I was fascinated that so much stuff could fit into such small spaces. And as soon as one was unloaded off it would go for another load.

"After about three round trips for each truck two late model Chevrolet station wagons pulled up jammed with people and more boxes. Children literally fell out of the cars once the doors opened. They began running in and out of the house until a loud female voice yelled, "Everyone stop! Into the house now!" From then on all moved with order, civility, and silence.

"My safe little world was under siege. I would no longer be the king of the wall. The Morarity's had arrived. All eleven of them. And in a few years Frank and Donny Morarity would introduce me to the virtues of tobacco and alcohol and pictures of naked women.

"I had been watching the smallest but not the youngest of my new neighbors. She was shorter than me but appeared to be about my age. And she was the hardest worker of the bunch. She wore a bright yellow sleeveless dress that made her look like a daisy with legs. She was barefoot. As I learned later shoes were a necessary evil that were discarded as soon as possible.

"She caught me looking at her and I felt like I had done something I shouldn't have. And as she walked across the street to lecture me on being a peeping tom, I wanted to run into the house but feared that cowardice in the face of imminent danger would permanently harm my future manhood. So, I sat my ground and waited for my punishment. Paying deference to what she had to say would be a big part of my life from then on.

"I couldn't take my eyes off of her as her bare feet moved with purpose and precision. Her arms swayed back and forth making the sides of her dress move in syncopated rhythm. As she stood right in front of me I expected a lecture but was amazed when she stuck out her hand and said, 'I'm Ellen Colleen Morarity. Nobody calls me Ellen Colleen except my mamma when she's mad at me. So, if you know what's good for you you'll just call me Ellen. Saw you looking at me. Figured you wanted to be friends.'

"I really didn't hear everything she said. Maybe I was mesmerized by her yellow dress. Maybe it was her curly red hair that fell wistfully to her shoulders. Or her moss green eyes that were as big as silver dollars. I don't know. But from that moment I was captured. She would become my best friend, my taskmaster, my cheerleader, my life-long companion. She would inspire me to do things I could never imagine. Find the best parts of me I never knew I had. Make me weep and rejoice because of her courage.   And she knew it, too.

"What's your name? Can't be your friend if I don't know what to call you."

"O. L."

"What kinda name is that? Nobody has just letters for a name. Really, what's your name?"

"Othello Lafayette. I waited for her to start laughing like all the other kids. But she just put her finger on her cheek and cupped her chin. And stood there thinking."

"That'll never do. Did your mother not love you or something? Were you an ugly baby? Why would she name you that?"

"I just stood there with my head hung feeling dumb."

"I know. I'll call you Blondie. I like that name. Yeah, Blondie it is."

"The funny thing was I didn't have blonde hair. Never. Mine was as black as coal. She just made it up right there. Just like that. Nobody knew why, not even Ellen. And from then on I was Blondie. And I never questioned it or her, something that would prove to be smart as I got older."

Ellen pretty much ran the family, which was fine with Blondie. She liked being in charge, and was very good at bossing others around. He wasn't. She was passionate and demonstrative and compelling. Quick to defend people of principles. Even quicker to forgive. He loved the way she could be filled with righteous indignation, especially when it was directed at those who took advantage of the ignorant, the innocent, and the lost. He was less forceful, less argumentative, preferring to avoid conflict and confrontation.

Christmas Eve on Deery Street was an event, one that involved the whole neighborhood. The tradition began because of their only son, the fourth of their seven children. Being a devout Catholic, Ellen named their six girls – Magdalene, Ester, Sarah, Mary, Naomi, and Ruth – for strong, courageous women in the bible. She named their son Franklin Abraham, after the two presidents whom she said saw the country through its darkest days.

Frank was a really bright, really big boy, taller, heavier, stronger than others his age. His hands were extraordinarily large, like they could wield a spike-driving sledgehammer as easily as his favorite Louisville Slugger. He was an imposing sight. Those who didn't know him were instantly intimidated. Those who knew him loved him because his heart was even bigger. He was forever championing the outcasts, those others made fun of, those who were always picked last or by default. His sisters would bring home stray animals. Frank brought home stray kids.

"Late one Christmas Eve afternoon I was sitting in the chair next to the window that looked out over the front porch and into the street. Ruth and I were reading the paper. Actually, I was reading the paper to her. She would stand in the crook of my arm as I held up the paper. She'd ask, 'What's this say, Poppa' or 'who's that in that picture.' But we'd always end up with the funnies. Her favorite was Little Orphan Annie. Sometimes she'd squat down on my lap in front of the paper so she could see Annie and Sandy better. Sometimes she'd say, 'Come on Poppa Warbucks. Let's see what's happened to Annie and Sandy today. That's how she learned to read. Every night standing in the crook of my arm. One hand holding the edge of the paper, the other around my neck."

"This particular Christmas Eve Naomi and I heard two sets of feet clomping on the front porch. We recognized one set as Frank's. About the time she got down to see who it was they burst in. Frank had another boy in tow by the sleeve of his too-big corduroy coat."

"Before anyone could ask, Frank blurted out, 'This is my new friend, Roger. He's visiting his grandpa on Luttrell Street 'cause his grandma died last year and his grandpa doesn't have anybody to have Christmas with because everybody lives someplace else. But his grandpa had to work tonight and he was just sitting out on the walk by himself. So I asked him what he was doing out there. And he said he was just waiting for his grandpa but he wouldn't be home 'till late."

This whole time Roger never looked up. He just looked at his shoes that were tied with several broken shoelaces. His hands and face were dirty. He looked lost.

"As Frank continued his expose of Roger's brief, little life, Naomi reached over and lifted his face. His right cheek had a red whelp along his cheekbone and his right eye was puffy. We later found out that Roger had just come to live with his grandfather to avoid an abusive father.

"Naomi, why don't you take Roger into the bathroom and help him wash his face and hands. Then see if there's not some milk in the fridge. Or maybe Mom might have some hot chocolate ready."

She took Roger's hand and without a word – and with that smile I both loved and dreaded because she knew that I couldn't resist it and because it would cast her spell on some boy someday who'd take her away from me – she and

Roger were off to clean up.

"Frank, you stay here. Ruth can take care of Roger. I want to talk to you. How come you brought Roger home? Does his mom know he's here?

"No sir. He's mom's not here. She's at their house in Alabama. It's just Roger and his grandpa. And his grandpa's at work. He was just sitting there shivering and crying. I didn't want to say he was crying in front of him. It might hurt his feelings and he looks like he's been hurt already."

"Why'd you bring him here?"

"Cause everybody's gotta have some place to go on Christmas Eve."

"From that moment on, Frank's admonition to me became the theme for every Christmas Eve – everyone has to have some place to go on Christmas Eve."

Roger bounced between his grandfather's house, his mother's house, and the Jones' house, which is where he preferred to live. There he was a member of the family. He would sometimes stay for months at a time. Sometimes years. He would sleep on a pallet made of quilts and pillows on the floor in Frank's room, which was a converted room in the attic.

As Roger got older his visits were less frequent and with less duration. He joined the army after graduating from high school. Ellen and Blondie both wrote him every week. He rarely wrote back. After he was discharged from the army he briefly visited a couple of times. The he disappeared and they never saw him again. Every five or six years he'd call. Roger wasn't much for keeping in touch.

108

The word quickly spread among their Deery Street neighbors. Then among neighbors on Luttrell Street, and Eleanor Street, and even streets that were just barely considered to be in the neighborhood. If you had no place to go or if you just want some company, 713 Deery Street was the place to be on Christmas Eve.

Over the years the Christmas Eve festivities grew into the Christmas event. Six o'clock was always the appointed time. Folks would line up at the front door. As the tradition grew the line got longer and longer, sometimes winding its way down the sidewalk and around the corner on Fifth Avenue. Most were neighbors, some weren't. But it didn't matter. Everyone was always welcome.

Blondie and Frank would greet them with a warm "Merry Christmas" and a firm handshake. Unfortunately for him, Frank always had to greet the old ladies who'd tweak his cheek and say things like "You're so sweet" or "What a big boy you're getting to be" or "Don't you look just like your mother." And it didn't matter how old he was, the same little old ladies would say the same thing every year.

Ellen and the girls would be busy keeping glasses and plates filled. And if any of the young men hung around the table too long visiting with one of the girls they'd get that look from her that shot daggers into their hearts. The girls would then hurry back into the kitchen. The boys would quickly leave the room if not the house. Ellen's reputation as a woman whose tongue and index finger could bring grown men to their knees whimpering for forgiveness was legendary.

In any given corner you could hear discussions about the sad state of affairs at city hall. Or all the juicy gossip fresh from the beauty parlor. There weren't many decorations in the house. The focal point was a floor-to-ceiling tree covered with homemade ornaments and what seemed to be thousands of multicolored lights. The house smelled of turkey

109

and cranberries and warm apple cider and fresh coffee. But mostly it was a place filled with the warmth of the season; filled with the hope and anticipation that Christmas brings; and filled with people who truly enjoyed being with each other.

The dining room table, where everyone served themselves, seemed to reach from room-to-room. It was made of Wormy Chestnut by the Pennsylvania Amish. It easily weighed five or six hundred pounds and was at least one hundred years old. Ellen's grandfather had won it in a poker game down on Front Street.

Front Street, which run along the North bank of the Tennessee River, was where you could get anything you wanted. Anything. Especially those things the law and society said were illegal or immoral. And you could find some things on Front Street nobody wanted. The riverbank was lined with barges permanently moored. On the barges were a variety of structures that housed a variety of activities. All were examples of the seedier, lustier side of life. Ellen forbid even the slightest mention of Front Street in her house, although Blondie would occasionally "wander around down there just to observe human nature" as he put it. No one spoke of his few Front Street excursions.

For the last few Christmases promptly at six o'clock he would assume his seat at the head of the table just as he had done for so many years. Sitting there alone brought back so many things, memories so clear and exact they could have just happened.

There was the year that Frank and Roger thought it would be fun to put laxatives in the brownie pan when Ellen wasn't looking. That year Santa brought surprises throughout the neighborhood.

There were several memories about Sarah, who fell in love with every boy who smiled at her. There was a standing bet to see if one boy could make it for two Christmases in a row. None had. Blondie said she'd grow up to be serial marryer.

There was the year Frank was in the war and Ellen stayed at Mass all Christmas Eve night lighting candles and praying for his safe return. Or the year when Magdalene left home with her new husband and created the first permanent vacancy at the table. And the year Ellen died seven weeks and two days before Christmas.

As he sat at the table remembering, without thinking he reached under the table and rubbed the carvings on the inside of the side panel. And he smiled. They were the initials of Magdalene and her first boyfriend that symbolized a right-of-passage created quite ceremoniously and passed down from Magdalene to her siblings.

His name was Jake Vaughn. Every facet of her fifteen-year-old life was consumed with Jake Vaughn, a boy three years older. His name or initials were written on everything Magdalene owned – homework, notebook, sneakers, papers all over her bedroom walls, the bathroom mirror, the inside cover of her bible. Jake was everywhere.

He was a leader-of-the-pack type. The kind fathers feared and mothers hated. He had a leather motorcycle jacket and the motorcycle to go with it, a Harley Davidson Duo-Glide they always heard but never saw. He always had a pack of Lucky Strike cigarettes rolled up in the sleeve of his white T shirt that also revealed a tattoo that read "Born to Raise Hell." Oh how she wanted her name to be surrounded by a heart, forever etched on Jake's upper arm.

They loathed the idea of their first born associating with an older boy who clearly has no ambition or social grace. Ellen rarely passed up an opportunity to express her displeasure about Jake. But they knew that if they forbid her to see him she'd just sneak around after him.

"He's just motorcycle trash," she'd say. "A hoodlum. He'll never amount to anything. Most likely wind up in jail before he's twenty. Or shot dead by a policeman while robbing someone's home. Probably outs. Boys like him only want one thing from girls, you know, young lade. And he's too old for you."

It came to her during one of Ellen's dinner lectures about Jake ruining Magdalene's and the family's reputation. Magdalene had reached down to retrieve her napkin from off the floor. It was instantly obvious what she must do.

Since there was no way to permanently inscribe his name on her body the next best thing, she thought, was to carve their initials under the dining room table. The table her family had owned for many years. The table her mother loved and almost worshipped as the symbol of family strength and stability. The table where her mother unleashed her Irish temper and venom on poor, sweet Jake. It would be a double blow – one for true love and one for defiance against tyranny.

Blondie discovered the "M. J. loves J. V." a few months later. But he kept it to himself. The truth came out during one of the spring cleaning marathons. Ruth, the youngest, was assigned to clean the table from top-to-bottom.

"Mamma come quick. Look what's written on the table."

Ellen rushed to the dining room horrified that someone would write on the table.

"Where? Where's the writing? I don't see anything." She was relieved to find that the tabletop had not been defaced.

"No mamma. Down here."

Ellen stooped down and found Ruth sitting under the

table, pointing to the eternal abbreviations of her sister's undying love. Ellen just looked at the carvings. Ruth sat there afraid to move. Ellen just looked at the initials. Ruth kept waiting for the famous eruptions from her mother. But when nothing happened she quickly scooted out the other side and ran to her room where she'd be safely out of range. Ellen remained in her half-sitting, half squatting position staring at the letters for several minutes. Then she stood and went back to the kitchen. And nothing was ever said about the initials neatly carved in her table.

When she felt it was safe to leave her room Ruth quickly and proudly spread the word of how she had lived to tell the tale of the Dining Room Table Massacre in two-part harmony. As the word spread each child was filled with the same courage and defiance that had prompted Magdalene to act. And over the years they each carefully, but only when no one was in the house, performed the same ritual, etching their initials underneath the dining room table. Except for Sarah, who was banned from initialing the table after the third set was discovered.

As his children became adults, they all moved away and had families of their own. The Christmas Eve tradition began to wane. One-by-one they stopped coming home for the holidays opting to have Christmas in their own homes rather than to travel to his.

Ellen had died a slow, agonizing death from cancer. And while it robbed her of her strength and her red tresses that reached to her waist and that she wore pulled back or in a giant three-strand braid, it never robbed her of her sense of humor. Or her passion for those who were on the outskirts of life. Or her unfaltering love and devotion for her children. And especially for Blondie, who was the only man she ever loved and the only friend she ever needed.

113

The neighborhood began to change, too. The other neighborhood kids who had been so much a part of his Christmas Eve for so many years were like his children, scattered across the country. His friends began to die or retire in Florida where the warm breath of the Atlantic soothed the pain of Arthritis and loneliness.

For the first few years after Ellen died his children and their families made an attempt to come home for Christmas. But they were never all there at the same time and they stopped coming after a few years. He, too, made some efforts to visit them but he always felt out of place. And it wasn't Christmas Eve unless it was on Deery Street.

Blondie was sitting in his easy chair next to the fireplace looking at the pictures of the grandchildren, all twenty-three of them, crammed next to each other on the oak mantel. Above the fireplace was a wreath woven with red and green plaid ribbons and adorned with three gold stars that hung from the bottom. Ellen and the girls had made it the first Christmas after Ruth was born. A string of Christmas cards hung from one corner of the mantel to the other. He stopped putting up the floor-to-ceiling tree the year after Ellen died. He still had a tree because it wouldn't be Christmas without one. But it couldn't be very tall though because the Arthritis in his shoulders kept him from decorating the top half.

Just as the grandfather clock in the hallway, which was always seven minutes fast, struck six times he heard what he thought was a faint, small knock at the front door. He looked out the small, rectangular window in the top of the door but didn't see anyone. But the knock sounded again. Opening the door he saw two small children, a boy and a girl. They couldn't have been more than four or five. They stepped back as he opened the screen door.

"Are you Blondie?" the boy asked.

They were fraternal twins. He clutched her hand. She clutched a small package wrapped in bright red paper with white ribbon around the corners.

"Yes, I'm Blondie," he responded as he stooped down so he could see their faces. "And whom might you be?"

"I'm Blondie, too. But that's not my real name. My real name is Othello Lafayette. But everyone just calls me Blond-ie. This is my sister, Ellen Colleen but she just goes by Ellen."

Blondie fell back, catching himself with both hands and sat in the doorway. He was speechless. All the years rushed before him as he watched the light from the Christmas tree dance in their eyes.

Ellen stuck out her hand with the small package. "You're supposed to open this now. It's your Christmas present from our daddy."

He took the present and began to unwrap it. Every seam had three or four layers of tape. They had obviously wrapped it. It was a 5 x 7 picture frame. As he sat there looking at the picture his heart raced. He could hardly breathe. It was a black and white picture of he and Ellen sitting on the front wall. Her mother took it the day they moved in across the street. It had disappeared more years ago than he could re-member. It was his favorite picture. Always would be.

"Blondie?" It was a familiar voice.

Blondie looked up and there stood Roger. The twins ran to him, each putting their arms around one of his legs.

"When I left for the army I took the picture. You and El-len took me in when no one else wanted me. You make me a part of your family. You were the only real parents I ever knew. I took the picture because it was the only one of both of you together. I keep it with me always. It has been with me all over the world. And every night I give thanks that Frank found me sitting on the wall and brought me here on Christmas Eve. I've been too ashamed to give it back.

"I'm rich. And I owe it all, everything I've done that's good in my life, to you and Ellen and Frank and the girls. I have no excuses for losing touch. When I learned that Ellen had died, I wanted to come but I couldn't bear to see you heartbroken. So, I'm here with my family to try and make tonight like it used to be."

Blondie was still speechless. Big tears streamed down his face.

"Okay, kids. You know what to do."

They each took one of his hands, helped him up, and led him to the front railing. Because he was listening intently to Roger he hadn't noticed that a crowd had gathered on the sidewalk in front of the house. Roger pulled a small flashlight from his pocket and turned it on. Instantly the sidewalk and street were filled with what seemed to be hundreds of tiny lights that flickered up and down Deery Street. There were friends and neighbors he hadn't seen in years with their children and grandchildren and great grandchildren.

Standing in front were all seven of his children. There was Magdalene and Jake, who was now a member of Congress. He still rode a Harley and he still smoked Lucky Strikes. And he did have a tattoo of a heart with Magdalene written in the center. While Ellen had been his greatest critic she also became his greatest supporter. When he first ran for Congress she raised over ten-thousand dollars, with each donation no more than fifty dollars. Most were twenty-five or less. And When she died Jake sobbed uncontrollably.

Frank stood next to Roger's wife. Sarah, the serial marryer, was with husband number five. In front of them, standing on the wall that had been such an important part of life on Deery Street were all of his grandchildren.

Roger stepped to the front of the railing.

"Blondie wants to know why you all are here."

And in unison they all roared, "Because everyone has to have a place to go on Christmas Eve!"

Nanny's Locket

She stood gazing out the front window remembering-looking at everything but looking at nothing.

The front porch was the home for the metal glider that creaked and groaned like the rusted hinges of a wooden gate. It endured many years of children trying to see how hard they could push with their little feet that just barely touched the wooded slats of the porch. The two oldest grandchildren, in a fierce display of summer boredom, actually did turn it over, resulting in six stitches across one's left eyebrow, and one less tooth for the other. That glider had heard more stories and a few lies, especially when her husband recounted all the giant fish he caught and the whales that got away, than she could ever remember.

The street had seen the world change from trolleys that clicked and clacked and sparked on their journeys to cars with almost ever modern convenience that filled the air with rumbles and fumes that made her cough if she sat on the porch too long.

She had stood in front of this particular window on Christmas Eve for many, many years. It was an annual vigil. Her reminiscing soothed the passing time, restored her spirit and still gave her a sense of awe for all she had seen.

For many years she always wore the same thing on Christmas Eve-a red small-weld corduroy jumper that fell almost to her ankles. It was plain yet purposeful, simple but elegant, at least as much as a corduroy jumper could be. She wore a starched, crisply ironed white blouse underneath that looked like it came straight from the laundry. Of course she would never send clothes to the laundry. That seemed "uppity." She always told her daughters and her daughters' daughters that "true elegance is alluring, yet understated."

Her fashion philosophy was stretched to its limit by the daughters that went to college in the sixties. Tie-dyed clothes and bell-bottomed pants were not permitted through the front door. The neighbors would surely think that her girls had become nothing but trash. How would she be able to face the women at the WCTU. Only reluctantly did she allow them to sneak in through the backdoor. It seemed better than having them strip down to their underwear in the backyard. Given the moral decadence of the youth of that era, she was always afraid that they wouldn't have on any underwear and that they would strip naked just to exert their newfound independence.

The only jewelry she wore with the Christmas jumper was her wedding band and a small, silver plated, heart-shaped locket that read "To Joy, Love Bill." It was the first thing her husband had given her some fifty-two years ago when they were first courting. She wore it always. It was her most prized possession. Her mother thought it was a cheap, tawdry trinket. But then her mother was more impressed with style than substance. A few years ago the locket, along with other personal items that had no value to anyone but her, was stolen by some neighborhood thugs. Some of the items were recovered but not the locket. She felt naked without it.

It was more than just a locket. It symbolized almost fifty years of living and loving. That locket had seen her husband through three wars. It had seen poverty and triumph. It had birthed babies and buried friends. It was all her hopes and dreams. It represented all she was and is.

She felt a tug at the bottom of her jumper. Then another tug from the other side. Then the back and forth tugging became a contest to see who could pull the fastest.

"Children, stop pulling on Nanny's dress. You'll stretch it all out of shape. What do you want." She continued to look out of the window, her breath creating window clouds as she spoke. She smiled as she remembered all of the times she had cleaned fingerprint faces and messages about her children's undying love and devotion to whomever was their love du jour.

"Pop's gonna tell us a story. We want you to come sit with us."

"I don't know if I'm up to a story tonight."

"He hasn't told us a story in a really, really, really long time. Please come sit with us. Please. Please. Please."

Their supplication was too much.

"All right, I'll come. But you have to help me keep him on the story."

She took these little angels, who usually weren't, by the hands. As she turned from the window, she saw the reflection on the whole family through the narrow brick and frame house. Much like the lost locket, everything important was there in one place.

The adult women were in the kitchen washing and drying the good china and silver. The men still sat at the dining room table drinking coffee from hand-made mugs, ones that had been in the family longer than anyone could remember. No one actually knew who made them or where they came from. They were easily four or five hundred years old. That's certainly what they had been lead to believe. The men were usually very good to help with the dishes. However, they were absolutely forbidden to handle the good stuff. They were lucky to even use the good stuff. It was one of Nanny's hard and fast, set in stone: *at no time is a man to do anything with the good china and silver*. It had always been a rule. It was not a gender issue; it was a clumsy issue.

The teenage grandchildren were seated, reluctantly, on the living room divan. Their arms folded across their chests, totally bored as if to say, "another of Pop's stories. I wonder how many times we've heard this one. Oh, boy! I can hardly wait!"

The pre-pubescent kids had gotten the green felt table pads from off the dining room table, and along with several patch-work quilts, ones that truly were family heirlooms, had made a pallet in the living room floor. They were very adept at making a pallet in the floor. It was where they would sleep when they would come and spend the night.

They would lie on their stomachs and lay their chins on their arms which were folded on top of old, clumpy down pillows. And talk for hours of fame and fortune, love lost and love found. The world was simple and understandable. It was a ritual reserved for only those who were worthy of the pallet. As the kids out-grew this nocturnal tradition, the vacancy could only be filled with those who had proven themselves. Permission must be given from the one vacating his or her spot. Pallet positions were deadly serious with equally deadly consequences.

Nanny will never forget the time she was awakened in the middle of the night by the screams of one of the younger children. Without even putting on her robe, which clearly indicated that someone was at death's door, she ran to the bathroom from whence the torturous screams were coming. She flung open the door and found the two oldest boys holding one of the younger boys upside-down by his ankles above the toilet. His pajama shirt was down over his arms and head. Part was on the seat, part was in the toilet. It seemed this young interloper had snuck into the pallet when no vacancy had been declared. They were simply teaching him the importance of the pallet position progression.

All the grandkids had taken their places. Nanny was sitting in her winged-back chair located closer to the front door, very close to where she was standing earlier. Pop's chair was a cain-bottom, ladder-back chair, the one that went with the cherry secretary that stood in the corner perpendicular to the front window. He would sit there for hours working crossword puzzles or filling out entry forms for every mail-order contest he could find. He'd never won anything, but he was convinced he would. And win enough money to retire in Florida and fish.

"Tell us our favorite story, Pop. Please?" came the request from the younger. The teenagers just sat on the couch in disbelief that they had allowed themselves to be talked into hearing Pop's worn-out stories one more time.

"Hold the phone" an expression he used a lot. "I can't tell all the favorite stories tonight."

Each group had a favorite. One everyone liked was how he lost his eye in a hunting accident as a boy. Midway through the story he would take out his glass eye and roll it around in his mouth, swishing it from cheek-to-cheek. One time he got choked, spit out the eye, which promptly rolled across the floor and down the furnace grate. Fortunately, it got stuck just under the grate. However, the impact of the eye hitting the floor after being jettisoned from his mouth cracked his eye straight across the middle. When he put it back in it looked like he had two eyes in one socket. The kids loved that.

"I want to tell you a story I've never told you before."

A new story, could this be? Really, a new story? The idea of a new story sparked everyone's interest. Even the delinquents on the divan.

Pop was smaller than average. His hair was salt and pepper, but hadn't thinned much at all. He wore octagonal shaped wire-rimmed glasses, ones he had had for years. He had permanent black circles under his eyes from years and years of working two and three jobs so that his children could go to college. He was not formally educated himself. But he and Nanny insisted that their children would be college educated. And they all were.

He was extremely intelligent, well-read, and articulate. He loved to read and he read anything. He was always the champion of the downtrodden, at least as much as their resources would allow. He was not very emotional, except when moved to extremes. He dearly loved his children and grandchildren.

Everything had gotten quiet. Even the adults were seated quietly around the dining room table. The word of a new story had spread throughout the house.

"It was Christmas, 1943. Times were hard. Even though the Depression was officially over, everyone around here still felt its effects. The war was raging in Europe and in the Pacific. Everyone hoped that the war would be over soon. And I was afraid because I knew if it wasn't over I would join the Army when I graduated from high school (something some of you ought to consider) and would be sent off to fight.

"I was sixteen and I had my first girlfriend. She was the prettiest girl in school. And I couldn't believe she liked me, too. The first time I saw her was the winter before. She was getting out of a big, black car with a shiny silver ornament on the hood, in front of the school. It had snowed the night before. We had to go to school when it snowed. You don't know how good you've got it.

"She started walking down the walkway toward some other girls who waited for her to catch up. For some reason she stopped, turned and looked in my direction. I thought

124

I was going to die. I dropped my books on purpose so I wouldn't have to look at her. Of course, the snow didn't help my homework any. I'm sure she thought I was a complete buffoon. And I was sure they were talking about my lack of coordination. As I watched her, she looked like an angel walking in the snow. And I fell desperately in love with her from that instant."

"Who was she? Did she fall in love with you too? What was her name?"

"Her name was Joy."

"That's Nanny's name."

"That's right. It was your grandmother."

Everyone had moved closer so they could hear.

"I carried newspapers in the mornings before school. And I bagged groceries after school. Whatever money I needed I had to earn myself. I had saved and saved so I could buy your grandmother something special for our first Christmas. I searched this town over for just the right gift. But everything I really liked was too expensive and what I could afford was cheap and tacky. I didn't know what I was going to do. Time was running out. Then I found it. The perfect gift."

"What was it? What was it?"

"It was a gold, heart-shaped locket with a gold necklace. It wasn't real gold, but she couldn't tell."

"You mean like the one Nanny used to wear?"

"It was the same one."

"The same one?"

"The very same one. Even though I had been in love with her for almost a year, we hadn't been dating for that long. Her present was to be a surprise. When I finally found what I wanted it was just two days before Christmas. Because I had to carry papers and work at the grocery store on Christmas Eve, I knew I wouldn't have much time to get it to her. And to make things worse, it snowed eight inches on Christmas Eve morning. I figured that my only course of action was to take the present by her house after I finished carrying my papers on Christmas morning. I knew that I might not be able to give it to her myself, but at least she would have it on Christmas. Christmas morning I hurried as fast as I could to finish my paper route. I wanted to give it to her first thing or at least have it there when she woke up."

"Gee, Pop, I didn't know you were so romantic," retorted his least favorite son-in-law.

This son-in-law was twenty-five going on fifteen. He was from a rich family in Boston. A pseudo-aristocrat. He wanted to go to an Ivy League school, but daddy had gone to one of the best schools in the south on an athletic scholarship. So, as fathers will do sometimes, he insisted that his son go to his alma mater. His son had no scholarship, just daddy's name. Pop's daughter met him in college. She was on full academic scholarship; something Pop never let him forget.

With a look that would stare-down Satan himself, Pop fired back, "There's a lot about me you don't know, young man. There's a lot you don't know, period." He said it with a grin. Some weren't sure if he was kidding.

"As I said, it had snowed the day before. About eight or nine, maybe ten, inches. The wind was blowing hard, so hard that I just couldn't roll the newspapers and throw them on the porches as I normally did. I had to put them behind the screen doors to keep them from blowing off."

"Pop, are you sure it was only ten inches and not ten feet.

And were you still barefooted because you couldn't afford shoes, like when you had to walk to school every day in ten feet of snow for fifteen miles with only a piece of bread and four crackers for lunch?" questioned one of the teenagers.

"Aw-right smart guy," he said with a grin. "You'd of never made it in my day. Do you want to hear this story or not?"

All answered "yes" in unison.

"It was bitter cold, about fifteen degrees. The wind swayed the leafless trees back and forth in a wistful wonderland ballet. The temperature had warmed just enough the day before to melt the snow on the sidewalks, which refroze Christmas Eve night. In fact, I fell several times carrying papers that morning. And each time, I fell squarely on my bottom. The seat of my pants had a wet spot that perfectly outlined each cheek. My nose was red and running. My eyes watered, the tears immediately freezing as they ran down my cheeks. I looked like an icicle with eyes. It took me about an hour to walk the two miles to your Grandmother's house.

"In those days houses were built very close together. I'd go out of my way to walk by hoping to catch a glimpse of her

"After trudging through the waist-deep snow (he looked at his captivated audience and chuckled out loud with his clever exaggeration) and ice and wind, feeling much like a postman, I finally got there. I noticed that the Christmas tree was the only thing lit in the house. The blue and green and red lights shown brightly through the window. And the light from a near-by street lamp made the tinsel and icicles sparkle like the stars just after the sun sets and the moon rises, the time when only they light up the sky. The sun was just below the horizon, casting a blue-gray blanket across the world. It was that time each day were we are still innocent, when life is simple, when fairy dust still sparkles on the eyelids of sleeping children.

"As I crossed the street I noticed someone sweeping the steps and porch of her house. I thought it was weird because the snow had already been cleared. It was a woman whose back was to me. She had just bent down to pick something up, so all I could see was from her butt down."

"How'd you know it was a woman, then?" The least favorite son-in-law never passed up a chance to get in a dig.

"Well since she had on a flower-covered house coat and lace around the bottoms of her pajamas, I figured it was either a woman or a really sweet man. I assumed the former. Anymore questions?"

Silence.

"Since she hadn't heard me approach, I stood at the bottom of the steps, not wanting to startle her."

"Excuse me, m'am."

"But I startled her anyway. I'm sure she didn't expect anyone to be at the bottom of the steps at that early hour. She stood straight-up, spinning around as she did. And as she did, she slipped on the slick porch and fell. There she sat. Her knees bent to about eye-level. Her hair was rolled with objects I'd never seen before (and still haven't). She had a bandanna that covered her ears, came up around the sides of her face, and tied in a knot just above her forehead. She looked like Rosie the Riveter in all those support the war posters. She was desperately trying to cover her night clothes with her robe that had come untied when she fell. But her hair never moved.

"She rolled over on her knees as lady-like as she could. She reached for the banister. But the banister wasn't as close as she thought. This time she ended up on her face, spread eagle on the porch. I hurried up the steps to try and help. Forgetting that the steps were slick, I tried skipping every

128

other step. However, I caught the toe of my foot on the top step. I fell too. You guessed it. I fell on her just as she was getting to her knees again. We both went to the porch with a very loud oomph. And there we were. Her lying face down; me lying on top of her. We were like two spoons in the silverware drawer. Two spoons in fifteen degree weather on the front porch. And her hair still hadn't moved.

"We lay there perfectly motionless. I thought she was dead. I wanted to be. Then she said calmly, matter-of-factly, 'young man, please remove yourself from off of me. And do so very, very slowly.' I did as I was told (something some of you should practice more often) and slowly eased myself off her. Once I was standing, I tried to help her. Of course, given my display of grace, she would have none of that. She stood, straightened her robe and then turned around and looked me straight in the eyes."

"Whom might you be, young man?"

"I'm Bill."

"Bill who?"

"I'm Bill. My Daddy calls me Billy." I couldn't remember my last name. I couldn't remember anything other than 'I'm Bill.'"

"Are you the young man that is trying to court Miss Joy?"

"I did manage to get out 'yes m'am' and not I'm Bill again."

"And what, may I ask, are you doing here at this hour?"

"I was frozen. I stood there expecting to have her broom rammed down my throat."

"I brought Joy's, I mean Miss Joy's Christmas present." I was just going to leave it behind the door (which really wasn't true). I was going to knock on the door and ask to see her. But I wasn't about to say that."

"Young man, young ladies do not receive gentleman callers at this hour. And they certainly don't receive them unannounced." I was shivering now from fear not from the cold.

"If you would like to come back at two o'clock this afternoon I'm sure she would see you then."

'Two o'clock. Yes ma'am. Yes ma'am, two o'clock.' "I turned carefully this time and got away as fast as I could."

"On the way home, I tried to figure out who this woman was. The best I could determine was that she must have been the maid. It made sense that Joy would have a maid; she rode to school sometimes in a big, black limousine looking car; she lived in a big house; the woman called her 'Miss Joy'; and no one except a maid would be out sweeping the porch and steps that didn't need sweeping. *Must be nice to have someone do your chores."*

"At fifteen until two, I stood at the bottom of her steps dressed in my best coat and tie, dress pants, hair slicked back with a little dab of Brylcream. The temperature had warmed some but it was still very cold. Given that morning's interlude with the maid, I wanted to ring the front door at exactly two o'clock. So, I stood at the bottom of the steps freezing my buns off for an extra fifteen minutes."

"At exactly two o'clock I rang the doorbell, which was promptly opened by the maid.. What a difference a few hours can make. This was not the same woman that had been face-down on the porch. Rosie the Riveter should look this good. She had on a flowing, empire-waist, crimson dress. She wore pearl earrings and a pearl necklace that scooped about six inches from the top of the dress (I later learned that the pearls were fake. A good fake, but fake neverthe-less). Her nails were finely manicured. She had classic facial features. And the radio transistors were gone from her hair."

"My name is Bill. May I please see Miss Joy, I mean Joy?" I don't know what it was, but I could never tell her my last name. I don't think that I ever did. The trauma of lying on top of an older woman must have been too great for my ado-lescent psyche."

"Yes, young man, I know you're Bill. Won't you please come in? I'll see if Miss Joy can see you now." She proceeded to go about half-way up the stairs. 'Miss Joy, a young gentle-man is here to see you.' Then she started back down the steps toward me. *Oh no, I'll have to talk to her. I can't tell her my whole name. How am I going to have a conversation?* I thought to my-self. By this time I had taken the present out of my overcoat pocket and was holding it with both hands in front of me."

"By now my front porch partner was standing in front of me. I could hear footsteps above me approaching the stairs. But not wanting this woman to think that all I could say was 'I'm Bill', I blurted out the first thing that came to mind."

"What's it like being a maid? Do you make pretty good money? I'm sure more than carrying papers and bagging groceries. Don't you get Christmas off? It doesn't seem fair to have to work on Christmas."

"She just stood there with her mouth open, glaring at me like she wanted to hang me by my bow-tie that my mother had to tie for me."

By this time Joy had appeared. 'Merry Christmas, Bill. I see you've already met mother.'"

"Mother?"

"Yes, young man. Mother, not maid. Mother."

I looked at the woman. Then looked back at Joy. Then back at the woman.

"Mother?" World War II was no longer a threat. I was going to die right there in the foyer of their house. I was speechless. I couldn't even say, 'I'm Bill'. Then I began speaking in tongues, dropped the present, ran out the front door, slipped and fell in about the same spot as before, and bounced down the steps and out into the street, which was now slushy from melting snow. I ran all the way home just mumbling mother...mother... mother.

"And that's the story of how Nanny got her locket"

Everyone looked at Nanny who was grinning ear-to-ear.

"What happened? Obviously, you overcame Pop's major faux pas," which came rather sincerely from the least favorite son-in-law.

"He avoided me for weeks. It was like he fell off the earth."

"I was humiliated. I couldn't bear to see her."

"One time at school, he even ducked into the girl's restroom when he saw me coming down the hall."

"So, what happened? I waited for him after his last class one day and literally push him against his locker and held him there with one hand and shook my finger at him with the other hand."

"What did you say? Did you yell at him? Did you smack him?"

"What I said was, 'Bill Roberts, quit acting stupid! I can't believe you've been avoiding me. I don't care about what happened.' I had the locket around my neck. I held it up right in his face. This is the most wonderful present I've ever received. I'll wear it always. Do you want me to be your girl or not?"

"What did he say?"

Pop reached in his coat pocket and pulled out a small, brightly wrapped package. He looked at everyone. "I said," then he looked at Nanny, "will you be my girl?" Then he handed her the gift. Nanny sat there. She seemed afraid to open the present.

Everyone, the least favorite son-in-law too, began saying, "Open it. We want to see what it is. Hurry! Open it."

She began pulling the taped edges away from the paper until it was all off. She lifted the lid of the small box. Tears began to stream down her face as she took out a gold necklace with a gold locket. The locket said, "To Joy, Love Bill." It was her locket. The house became perfectly still, perfectly silent.

Pop spoke. "Last month when I was raking leaves I thought I noticed something shining in the grass. So I raked harder and this is what I found. Apparently, the thugs dropped it and then stepped on it, burying it in the soft, wet soil. So I took it and had it cleaned up."

He then took the locket and placed it around her neck. And kissed her on the forehead.

Everyone had gone. The house was silent. No more sounds of radio controlled cars running into table legs or people legs. She was again standing in front of the front window gently rubbing the locket between her thumb and index finger like she had done for so many years. She didn't notice that Pop was standing behind her. He bent over her shoulder, blew his breath on the window making a big cloud on the glass. He took her hand, closed all her fingers except one. And with both of their fingers he wrote, "To Joy, Love Bill."

Magic Socks

Luke Hollister's Christmas would be a test, one that would require cunning, strength, and skill with a needle and thread. Failure would land him, he was certain, on the all-time terrible father's list.

Through quirks in DNA and evolution, Luke had been blessed with two sets of twins, female and male. Maggie and Mona were high school seniors and were known simply as "the girls." They were cute, funny, and at the top of their class. Everyone, especially boys, wanted to be around them. He had a great relationship with them. But they outgrew him a long time ago.

Jeff and Josh, known as "the boys," were lost in some parallel universe populated by adolescent boys and known only to them. The girls always referred to them much more descriptively. Their prowess and dexterity playing "Call of Duty" was spoken with reverence and awe in the halls of Eddy Junior High School. But they couldn't do the simplest tasks around the house without breaking something. When they talked to girls they spoke some strange language only Swahili witchdoctors could understand. Everything was confusing and uncertain in their lives. But there was one thing about which they were certain. Their father had an IQ of twelve. And since he'd been around since dirt, it was obvious that he understood nothing about their lives.

"Daddy? Daddy? Are you awake?" came this small, half whimpering voice; a sound that usually meant he was about to become arbiter or executioner in the very near future.

He rolled over toward the outside of the bed. Opened one eye, still unsure if the voice that had interrupted his sleep was part of a dream or real. Just as he thought, Katie, the youngest of his five children, was squarely eyeball-to-eyeball.

"What's the matter, sweetheart? What time is it anyway?" Things were too quiet to be very late

"It's early."

"How early?"

"It's pretty early."

"Exactly, how pretty early is it?"

"Exactly?"

"Yes, exactly! Why are you crying C'mere and tell me all about it."

By this time he had wiggled out from under the covers and was propped-up against the headboard. He raised his arm, and as if on cue, she snuggled in beside him, one arm around his back, and the other around his stomach. She laid here head on his chest. He began combing her hair with his fingers gently moving through the tangles from the night's sleep.

He thought of all the nights he had done the same thing after his wife died. And all the times Katie had awakened in the middle of the night. And how she had found safety there. And how he found safety with here there. They knew the routine by heart and did it without thinking, just as they were now.

"I'm not really upset crying. I'm mad crying!"

"Mad about what?"

"I can't find my special, magic Christmas socks. I bet those dumb boys hid them on purpose. They'd do that you know."

Originally, the socks were red with white, frilly lace around the top. The Littlest Angel was sewn on the outside of each ankle. They were Christmas socks like all Christmas socks found in any Walmart. In fact, that's where they got them. They didn't cost much. But then most magical things don't.

Now, the socks only vaguely resembled what they used to look like. One angel had come off in the wash; the other was barely hanging on by her halo. Neither was red anymore. One was dull pink. The other was sort tie-dyed pink and white, with occasional beige spots, the result of unexpectedly being bleached. A sin for which he had only recently been forgiven. They were too small, barely coming to her ankles. Her middle right toe was beginning to protrude through the seam. The left heel was half gone. But she wouldn't part with them. She wore them on every special occasion – Christmas, Easter, and Fourth of July. It didn't matter. And always when she performed. They were her magic socks.

"Now, sweetie, I don't think the boys would do that. And besides, you can't jump to that conclusion like that."

"Sure I can!" She was right. They would do something like that.

"I've gotta find my socks. I've just gotta!" Tears began to flow rather freely.

"I know the socks are special. And we'll find them. But why are they so important right now, especially this early in the morning?"

"If I don't find my socks I'll forget my lines in the play

tonight. Or my halo will fall off. Or something else awful will happen. And everybody will laugh at me. I'm the most important angel you know."

Luke understood the magic in special socks. He had a pair. They were the pair he had on when he hit his first homerun in little league. From that moment on he refused to wear any others. Or wash them. The magic was in the brown rings around the ankles created from red clay dirt mixed with sweat. He was convinced of two things: the bigger the rings, the better he would play; and if his mom washed them, the magic would be gone. And he would be forever doomed to baseball oblivion and anonymity. Never to hit the World Series winning homer for the Yankees in the bottom of the ninth. Never to succeed Mickey Mantle. Or hear him say "Nice catch, Kid."

It became quite a challenge to keep his mom from exorcizing the magic from the red clay rings he had worked so hard to gain. It became a game of hide-and-seek that whole summer. She obviously knew nothing about the finer nuances of athletic prowess.

The past few Christmases had been half-hearted for Luke. His wife's suicide left him unprepared and unaccustomed to being both father and mother, something fate or God had viciously and surprisingly inflicted on his ordered, predictable life.

They had not been at their own home since her death. Both sets of grandparents welcomed the opportunity for them to come visit at Christmas. He rationalized that both their parents shouldn't really be traveling. And it gave the kids a chance to spend time with their grandparents. But more than anything, he could deflect the pain and fear of knowing he couldn't make Christmas like it had always been. He would rather endure the hassles of getting everything done early, packing, and driving six hours with the offspring of Attila-the-Hun. Nothing would be screwed-up or left out.

The first trip taught him valuable lessons. Women with tiny bladders have children with tiny bladders. He also learned that four-out-of-five dentists recommend that people over forty should not listen to Toad the West Sprocket or Hooty and Blowfish. It had something to do with extreme teeth grinding. He had questions about the fifth dentist. Probably too much Nitrous Oxide.

At first, the kids understood not being at home for Christmas. But the novelty of a grandparents' Christmas wore off quickly. Luke understood their frustration and disappointment. They were away from their friends. The girls had boyfriends who had apparently moved into his house like thieves in the night, an appropriate term given the quadrupled grocery bills since the girls were once again in "true love." Compared to their past boyfriends, these boys actually weren't too bad. They had some manners, except at the table. They called him sir. He liked that. They occasionally used multi-syllabic words. And they had exquisite taste in earrings. The boys didn't like being with anyone except other pubescent boys.

Each year became increasingly more difficult to get them to agree to his Christmas retreat. He had promised this year they would wake up in their own beds on Christmas morning. He had broken several promises to them. He would not break this one.

"Daddy," her voice smaller now. "Will you help me find my socks?"

"Sure I will. As soon as we have breakfast we'll look for them. Is that Okay?"

She nodded her approval. "I'm gonna go look in the boys' room."

"Don't go in there right now. You'll wake them up."

"So! They'd do it to me."

"That's not the point. Just because they're inconsiderate doesn't make it right or that that's the way you should be. Besides, I don't want you going in there alone. It's too dangerous without an armed guard. Why don't you search your room again? You know, sometimes we look for things so hard and we want to find them so badly that we look right over them when they've been right in front of our face the whole time."

"Okay, I'll look again." Which was accompanied by a this-is-a-waste-of-time-but-I'll-do-it-to-make-you-happy look.

Striding determinedly, off she went. A woman with a mission, mumbling, "I'll find the socks or I'll kill the boys."

The kids were at the ages when they were gone all the time. The girls were eighteen and basically had their own lives. He mostly provided car keys, and a place for cheap dates. He wasn't sure what the boys did. He just knew he had to take them a lot of places or they could "never achieve their ultimate level of cool." Saturday mornings were the exception – they had breakfast together. It was sacred. Ah yes, how everyone had grown to love these times of family festivities and fun, these moments of concern and compassion, these times of endearment and enjoyment that came when his children gathered, gratefully seeking the knowledge and wisdom imparted by father-dear at the kitchen table.

The kitchen was filled with kaleidoscopic, rainbow splashes refracted by what seemed to be hundreds of pretend stained glass figures. They were hung with nylon fishing line from the top of each window. They gave the appearance they were floating, celestial objects frozen in their orbits. Over the years, each child had hung several. And always with pride and wonder in their accomplishment. The air was laced with a mixture of scents: the greasy, salty smell of bacon; homemade biscuits straight from the oven, the kind that are as much fun to make as they are to eat; and the aroma of freshly ground coffee that serpentines throughout the house and lingers for a while.

He sat at the table staring at the aftermath of family breakfast. The original Saturday Rule stipulated breakfast at home, prepared on a rotating basis among the natural groupings of the family – Maggie and Mona, Jeff and Josh, he and Katie. However, a broken window from a plastic butter; a humongous charred place in the kitchen floor caused by flipping over a skillet to smother the flames allegedly caused by a mysterious, unknown scientific phenomenon; and another small fire that only burned half of one side of the kitchen curtains has exempted the boys from culinary creations. They ate out when it was their turn.

Luke sat at the table overwhelmed with the symbolism before him. Too much had happened. Too little time. Too much to do. Too little energy. He had never truly done Christmas. Never cooked the whole meal. Never helped everyone with their shopping. Or all of the decorating. Or whole-house cleaning. Or addressing the Christmas cards. He'd done some of everything. But never all at once. He had mostly observed and enjoyed. And this year he had to help Katie get ready for the annual Christmas pageant.

The faint trills of a distant angel snatched him from his holiday self-pity. He traced the source to the smallest of their four bedrooms. Katie's room. She was singing as she searched slowly but meticulously through a pile of clothes. It was obvious the magic socks had not been found.

Katie had perfect pitch and almost a photographic memory. She had a truly beautiful voice, one any adult would be proud to have. It could be big and powerful or soft and disarming. It was very strange to hear such a mature, extraordinary voice coming from such a small girl. Folks came from all over to hear her sing. Each note was as clear as the sounds from the creek that rushed past a friend's mountain cabin on its way toward the fire-hued mountains that touched the sky, the place where they spent their mid-August vacations. He knew someday she would make princes cry and paupers smile.

"Hi, sweetie."

"I still haven't found my magic socks."

"Where have you looked?"

"I've looked everywhere. I really don't think the boys took them. They're not that stupid. They know how important they are to me. Any they know you'd kill them real bad. I'm scared I won't find them."

He sat down in front of her, crossed his legs Indian-style, just as she was sitting. They were separated only by the array of ten-year-old paraphernalia piled in the middle of the floor.

"You know, Katie, I had a pair of magic socks once. I wore them to plan baseball in. I always wore them. I used to hide them from Grammy so she wouldn't wash them."

"Didn't they stink real bad?"

"As a matter of fact, they did. But I didn't care. They had dirty brown rings around the ankles. That was where the magic was. I just knew if Grammy washed them, then all the magic would be gone. And I wouldn't be able to play anymore. Or at least that's what I thought."

"Did you play in them forever?" She said hoping the answer would be yes.

"Let me ask you a question. What socks did I have on last summer when I played ball?"

"I guess you had on the socks Maggie and Mona gave you for Father's Day one year. You know the ugly ones that fall down around your ankles."

"That's right. So I didn't have on my magic socks, then, did I?"

"No, I don't guess you did."

"How'd I play?"

"Okay, I guess. But I don't really remember. The boys kept pouring dirt down my underwear."

"Since you don't remember, I played really well. And I did it without my magic socks."

"That's different."

"How's it different?"

"I don't know. It just is." She was about to cry, afraid she was right and it was different.

"Katie, there's a lot of magic in the world. It's everywhere. But it's not in socks, or dirt rings, or littlest angels sweetie. It's in people. It's down deep inside. In our hearts. It's in the dreams you think about when you lay in the grass in the summertime and trace the Big Dipper with your finger. It's in all of us. When you sing, it's magical. Your voice makes an invisible cloud that surrounds everyone that hears you. And we feel warm and wonderful inside."

He knew she was afraid to believe him. She always had her socks.

"I'll forget my part. Or I'll sing bad notes."

"You won't forget your lines and you won't sing bad notes. But just in case, if you should forget something then just tell us your part in your own words. You know the story of Baby Jesus by heart. You'll know what to say. We'll keep looking for the socks. Just remember, Katie, the magic's in you, not the socks. And no matter what, I'm proud of you and I love you just because you're you."

The church sanctuary was filled with parents and grand-parents and all manner of relatives and friends, each adorned with some form of photographic equipment. All were there to hear her. Special events were really big deals.

Katie was one of those that thought she was late if she wasn't an hour early. Because she was the most important angel, they were at the church before anyone, including the custodian. She said it was so she could get her "mental mind" properly prepared for a performance that would" make the Baby Jesus happy." He knew better. The socks had not been found. She was hoping for some kind of divine intercession. This was, after all, the season of miracles.

Luke forced the boys to come. But he agreed to let them sit with two fourteen year old girls and their parents. It was most definitely uncool to sit with him. While it was uncool to be sitting with anyone's parents, anywhere, sitting next to the prettiest girls in their class more than compensated for their social faux pas. All the other boys would clearly see how studly they were.

The older twins had dates. Their plans didn't include the Christmas pageant. "I'll save four seats just in case" which brought a "Get real" in unison.

He was seated where Katie had requested – left center section, four rows back, isle seat. She just had to be able to find him, especially since she didn't have her magic socks. In fact, she had on no socks. She was taking no chances.

"Sir? Are these seats taken?" It was a familiar but out of place voice.

"I was saving these, but I guess they're not com...."

It was the girls. With their Siamese courtesans, who looked none-too-happy, firmly in-tow.

Mona bent over and whispered "Scoot over. We want to sit with you." When they were younger, they always demanded that he sit between them. His wife had to sit between the boys. She was more graceful stepping over people when the boys had to be escorted out during performances. She hadn't seen the end of many things.

"I thought you had other plans?"

Maggie answered this time. "We did. We changed our minds. You're not the only one who loves to hear Katie sing, you know."

"The goons don't look very happy." He called all their boyfriends goons. They were offended at first. But they had grown to recognize that boyfriends symbolized that one

145

day, some boy would take them away. And he would be left, again.

"We gave them the choice, go to the pageant and be with us. Or don't go to the pageant and don't be with us. Ta-dah!"

They both leaned close. "It's great having power over men, Dad!" they said with supreme confidence.

Luke leaned forward and glared at their wimpy little boyfriends. And grinned an ear-to-ear grin, one that said, "And you thought you could replace me. HA! Guess I showed you. Thought you could horn in on my territory, did ya? Think again, dudes!"

He took each of their hands, squeezed them and thought, *That's my girls.*

It was just about time for the big scene. The one where the most important angel was to proclaim to the shepherds the arrival of the Christ child. He was anxious. Really anxious.

A small group of shepherds clad in bright, vertical striped bathrobes, towels in corresponding colors tied around their foreheads, had gathered at one side of the stage. They rubbed their arms and hands over a few logs with fake fire to warm themselves. A multitude of stars, some with four points, others with five or six; some big, some little hung all over the blue velvet curtains behind them. In the middle was one giant, glorious star that out-shown the others. They paternally watched their flock of cotton-ball covered cardboard sheep and talked quietly among themselves.

Then there she was. Walking toward the shepherds. But something was wrong. Her halo had slipped to the side of her head, part of the garland hung down to her shoulders in a shiny, silver loop. And she hadn't noticed. Put off to the very last minute, they had made it out of a coat hanger that afternoon. And as usual, there wasn't enough time to do it properly.

With every step, the halo slipped a little more. She stopped mid-stage and faced the audience. The halo was barely on, much like the remaining angel on her magic socks. His heart was pounding. He wanted to run on stage and fix it.

"And there were in the same country, Shepherds, abiding in the field, keeping watch over their flocks by night," she spoke clearly, confidently.

The halo had held its place so far. *Please, please, please,* he kept thinking to himself.

Then the angel chorus proclaimed, "And lo, the angel of the Lord came upon them. And the glory of the Lord shown round about them. And they were so afraid. And the angel said unto them..."

She had moved in front of the shepherds. Gracefully, she raised her arms as if to gather the flock.

"Fear not..." As she began to speak, the halo fell to the floor and rolled to the edge of the stage. Well out of immediate reach. His heart sank. All the color rushed from her cheeks. A collective gasp ricocheted antiphonally throughout the sanctuary. Then silence. Tomb silence. His heart was racing. He felt very sick.

Katie stood motionless, frozen in her fear-of-fears. Her eyes found him. She was lost. She knew it. He knew it. She slowly lifted the hem of her angel's robe and looked down at her bare feet.

"No socks. No socks," she kept mumbling softly.

He too, was speaking softly. "The magic's in you. The magic's in you" over and over. Her eyes found his again. And everyone else disappeared into a blurry shadow. Just like all the times it was just the two of them. She was still speaking softly but instead of "no socks" she was saying, "Not socks. Not socks. Tell the story!"

She smiled her impish smile, the one that spoke a thousand words. The one that covered her face every time he asked her to sing. Luke sat back in his seat. Some great magic was about to be worked.

Katie whirled on the ball of one bare foot, the silence shattered by the sound of her unsocked feet running on the hardwood stage.

"Get up! Get up!" she yelled as she ran toward the shepherds who were now frozen, not knowing what to do with this change in script.

"The most wonderful thing is about to happen. You're gonna miss it. God's Son, The Baby Jesus, is about to be born. It's the greatest thing ever. His Mom and Dad are in Bethlehem, just around the corner. Don't be scared. God sent me to get you. He wants you to be there. It's really important. It's not far. C'mon!"

Everyone – the shepherds, the audience – everyone was stunned. She was running around the shepherds pulling on their arms, trying to lift them up, pushing them forward. Trying her best to herd them, and their sheep, toward Bethlehem just around the corner.

"C'mon! C'mon, it's the coolest thing ever. You gotta hurry. Tell everyone you see. And if you see some old guys with beards and towels wrapped around their heads carrying packages, bring them too. They gotta see The Baby Jesus, too. Let's go! Let's go!" Then she smacked the shepherd leader on the butt and off they went.

The audience roared and laughed and clapped thunderously as the "most important angel" led the way to Bethlehem just around the corner.

Mary held the Baby Jesus, gently swaying the heavenly bundle in her arms back-and-forth, back-and-forth. Joseph, the shepherds, with their cotton-ball sheep, and the old guys with beards and towels wrapped around their heads, watched silently. And in the silence, the most important angel appeared above them all.

She found him once again. Smiled that grin again. Closed her eyes. Took a deep, deliberate breath. Without warning, without accompaniment, she began.

"Oh holy night. The stars are brightly shining..."

The universe had become very small, very focused, there, standing above The Baby Jesus. Life and living had been reduced to their simplest terms in the innocence and power of this giant voice from this small girl that reverberated over and over and over.

"Fall on your knees. Oh hear the angel's voices...." Each note, each word as clear as could be.

Tears streamed down his cheeks. She was singing for him. And God was singing for everyone.

She had never sung like this before. Never! Her melody covered them all like the thin grey blanket that settles between ridges and mountains at day set, the day's last breath just before it slips into the anonymity of night. They were all mesmerized by the magic and majesty of this ten year old baby Jesus, this most important angel with-no-socks.

149

Everyone had settled into their nocturnal routines. The big kids were piled-up on the couch in the den watching some mindless dribble on TV. Jeff and Josh were in their room saving the world from all manner of alien invaders.

He sat on the top step of their wrap-around front porch. He held a cup of coffee in both hands, steam shimmering upward like smoke from his father's pipe. He was still absorbed by Katie's performance, one that rivaled any he had ever seen.

He felt something brush against his coat. He turned. It was Katie.

"Whadda ya doing out here? Aren't you cold?" She sat down beside him.

"No, not really. I was just thinking about how very proud I am of you. You were simply amazing."

She just smiled.

"Sweetie, I'm really sorry about the halo. It was my fault that it wasn't made very well. Will you forgive me?"

"For what?"

"For not being a better mother. I really try. But it's real hard." His voice was about to break.

She stood up. Moved down a few steps so she could look straight at him.

"We know you do. But we don't want you to be both. We just want you to be you. When I was standing up there tonight, right when my halo fell off, I've never been that scared in my life.

"I know. I was too."

"Then I saw you. And I could tell what you were saying. And I remembered about the magic. It was true. And it's true for you, too. But you won't let yours out because you think you have to be Mom. Well, she took hers with her. So, yours is all we have. And it's all we need.

Out of the mouths of babes, he thought.

"I have a present for you. It's not a Christmas present. It's just a special Dad present. Here, open it."

He slowly pulled the taped corners open from the ends of the small box wrapped in newspaper. On top was a note that said, "I don't need these anymore. The magic's in people." Underneath the note were her Magic Christmas Socks.

A Place to Go on Christmas Eve

The Angel with the Gold Tooth

The sign said "HOME" with and arrow pointing out to the tracks. It was just a plain cardboard sign, handmade, tapped above the door that opened out to the loading platform. I wonder if I'll ever get there.

Sam Kennedy sat in the middle of Union Station. He had been sitting in the same place for hours. Just looking and sitting, sitting and looking. He watched as people passed on their way to somewhere else. So was he, on his way somewhere else. On his way home for the first time in three years.

He sat perfectly erect – back straight, hips, knees, ankles at ninety degree angles. His uniform was virtually unwrinkled, a minor miracle since he had been traveling in it for almost three days now. He took great pride in his appearance. His grandmother, who lived in their home most of his life, always said, "A man's appearance is like a mirror; people see the reflection as the truth even though it may actually be hidden on the other side of the glass. Be neat, straight, and clean. It goes a long way." He took her advice to heart at an early age.

He was a sight to behold. A poster-boy for the army. A real life, honest-to God war hero, with rows and rows of ribbons and badges. On his sleeve was a round, red patch with a black hour glass in the center for the 7th Infantry.

He was a strikingly handsome young man. Jet black, wavy hair. Six foot two, one hundred eighty-five pounds. Well, he used to weigh that. He had big, warm, cow eyes, ones that melted the hearts of all the girls he met. Their mothers, too. Folks liked him instantly.

Everywhere he went people stared, their eyes drawn to

his colorful uniform. He had never gotten used to it, especially now. He felt self-conscious and uncomfortable. He neither thought of himself as handsome nor as a hero. He didn't like attention which was hard when he was the one everyone wanted to be around.

He was twenty-three going on a hundred. He had been thrown into a role far beyond his years, far beyond his imagination. He was lost somewhere between innocence and cynicism, between expectation and resignation, between dreams and dread. He wasn't sure what to feel or think or believe anymore. He was mostly tired and alone. And stuck in Union Station in Chicago on Christmas Eve. A long way from Duncan, Oklahoma. A long way from home. And a long way from Jessie.

"Cap'n. Cap'n. You alright?"

Leroy Brookins was a big barrel-chested black man who was a custodian at Union Station. He always wore bib overalls and a white shirt and tie underneath. "Just cause I's a janitor don't mean I can't look presentable," Brookins (no one called him Leroy) was prone to say. "I wares these overalls 'cause they has lotsa pockets. And they fits my big belly." He wore an old faded Fedora. At one time it was a medium gray whose brim was neatly blocked. Now it had several black rings just above the band from years of sweat. He kept it pushed down just above his eyebrows when he was working. But if he stopped to talk he would always push the brim up to his hairline. "If a man won't let you look him in the eye when he's talkin' to ya, ain't worth wasting your breath, can't trust 'im. Ain't worth talkin' to."

Like Sam, Brookins was one of those people that everyone warms up to immediately. His eyes sparkled like stars. His smile was ear-to-ear that showed brilliantly white teeth, with one gold tooth right in the middle.

"Scuse me for sayin' so, Cap'n, but you sho is a long ways

away. Is somp'n the matter?"

"This was to be my first Christmas home in three years. I was going to ask my girl to marry me. Don't have a ring yet. I don't have much of anything, really."

Sam was to have caught the eight-forty train to Oklahoma City the night before. But an s expected snow storm had delayed all transportation all across the Great Plains. Nothing was moving in or out of Chicago. He had been in Union Station since noon the day before. He had no idea when he would get home. He kept telling himself, what's a few more days after all you've been through. *Jessie'll be there when you get there.*

Brookins sat down beside Sam on one of the arched, double-sided passenger benches. He leaned back against the bench. Pushed the brim of his hat back. Clasped his hands on top of his giant belly.

"How long she been your girl?"

"Since the ninth grade. She's the love of my life"

"She love you like you love her?"

"Yes, she does. She wrote me every week. Sometimes two or three times. She kept me going. I kept her picture with me always. Some of her letters, too. And after I got hurt I read them every day in the hospital. It was like she was my guardian angel."

Jessie was statuesque at 5'11". She was strikingly beautiful. Long raven tresses, and eyes as blue as the Pacific. She had an infectious laugh and a disarming smile. Sam knew how lucky he was.

For some reason Sam felt an instant kinship with Brookins. Like they shared something of importance. Something that helped define who they were.

"Love's a great thing. It makes us better than we think we can be. But it brings out the devil in us, too. It makes us do things we wouldn't do most of the time, sometimes good, sometimes not. Take this gold tooth – had the real one pulled and this gold one put in to try and make a woman like me. Said she really liked shiny things. Thought this would really get her. And with my natural beauty and charm how could she resist?" Brookins chuckled out loud.

"So, what happened?"

"Laughed at me. Said I wuz fat and dumb. Said she wouldn't go out with me if I had a mouth full of gold. Cost me a month's pay. Man, the things we do to please women. I got the last laugh, though. Wish I had a dollar for every kid that smiled back at me after I flashed this here golden ornament. Yes sir, can't buy that kinda joy."

"What happened to her?"

"She wuz showing out at some fancy party. Stepped on the hem of her dress. Fell down some steps. Knocked out her front teeth." Brookins could hardly contain himself. "Didn't have 'nough money to get 'em fixed, much less to have gold ones put in. Just a big gap, now. Whistles when she speaks. Makes a real high pitch, the kind that makes dogs howl. Corse, when she talks everybody has to look to see where that awful sound's comin from. Yes sir, the Lord sho do work in mysterious ways."

Brookins stood up, pushed his hat back down to his eyebrows. He was still reveling in having been victorious. "Life has a way of making things even," he said as he walked away.

And off he went. Not really walking, sorta shuffling and dancing at the same time. It was as if his feet were barely touching the floor.

Brookins stopped regularly to check on Sam, each time offering some tid-bit of wisdom about life. "Seems to me Christmas is 'bout lightin' the darkness. There's light in your life now. Not that terrible darkness you wuz in overseas. The wonderful girl you talk about all the time will be with you sooner than you think. I see how your face lights up when you think of her. Yes sir, Cap'n, Christmas is 'bout being in the light. 'Bout Jesus light."

Minutes seemed like days. The hours drug by. And as they did, Union Station increasingly became more and more deserted. Union Station was like a banquet room in a castle. Ornate trimmings, intricate inlays in the marble floors. Giant chandeliers hung from the ceiling in succession up and down corridors that seemed to go on forever.

He had watched throngs of people for a day and a half come in and out of the platform doors on their way home. Many spoke to him as they passed. Most smiled. Some spoke. Others, primarily other soldiers and children, stop to chat for a few minutes. Mostly army talk: "Where were you stationed? What unit were you with? Did you see much action? What's those ribbons stand for?"

A young mother with two young boys in tow smiled and spoke as they walked by. "Your daddy's a soldier like that young man" she said. The boys stopped, fascinated by all of the stuff on Sam's uniform.

"Hey, mister. How come you're wearing a necklace? Soldiers don't wear necklaces. They're for girls." The mother apologized for her son. Smiled again, then drug them off by the arms. Sam could hear her admonitions in between the clomps of the boys' heal on the marble floor.

The necklace the boy referred to was actually two strips of blue cloth that circled his neck and fastened in the back. In the front, just below the knot of his tie, they formed an octagon with white stars in rows. Below the stars hung a gold eagle clutching a gold star encircled by a wreath. It was the only medal he wore.

Although he had spent most of the time sitting, he would occasionally walk around to stretch his legs. Sitting for long periods of time made them hurt worse than normal. But he felt self-conscious because he walked with a pronounced limp. He wasn't embarrassed or ashamed. He just didn't want to draw attention to himself. He had been wounded three different times. Fortunately, his scars were hidden under his uniform.

Sam had spent the last Christmas at Walter Reed Army Hospital convalescing from his last injury. The two before that were spent in Kumwa and Chorwan Valleys along the thirty-eighth parallel. He was just now coming home. What had helped him progress at a fast pace was the thought of spending the next Christmas with Jessie and his family. Not at Walter Reed again. No, he was going to be with Jessie on Christmas Eve. And he would ask her to marry him. All of that energy and pain dedicated to being home by Christmas Eve only to be snow-bound in Chicago. Where he knew no one except Leroy Brookins.

"Tell me something, Leroy. How long have you been a custodian here?"

"Now, Cap'n, I told you not to call me Leroy. Only them that ain't my friends or bill collectors call me that. My friends calls me Brookins. You my friend ain't ya?"

"Yes. Sorry."

"First off I's a janitor. Don't know nutin' 'bout being no custodian. Janitors scrub toilets. That's what I do. Guess I been working here 'bout thirty-five years. Yeah, that's right. Came here right when I got out of the Army in 1918. Kinda like you, I suppose."

"So, you were in the first big one."

"Yup. Saw lots of action. Men dying everywhere. Made some great friends, though. Still keep in touch with some of 'em. Even after all this time. War's a lot like love in some ways. Makes you do things ya never thought you could. Some you never thought of. Some good, some bad."

Sam was shaking his head in agreement and remembering as Brookins spoke.

"Take that medal around your neck. Bet you never thought you'd ever have anything like that."

"No, Brookins, I never thought that I'd have something like this. We were all boys. All scared. Jessie kept me going."

"See what I mean about love and war. They's a lot alike, Cap'n. A lot alike."

"Brookins, is there a restaurant close by that might be open? I'm really hungry."

"Well, Cap'n, let me see. Most places gonna be closed by now. There's the Embers, though. It's really swanky. I hear tell the food's real good, especially the steaks."

"A good steak sounds great. Is it close by? Would you honor me and be my guest for dinner?"

Brookins was visibly moved by Sam's offer. He had only known Sam for a day. And he wasn't used to being invited to dinner at fancy restaurants, especially by white people.

"Thank you very kindly, Cap'n, for you offer. But I better stay right here." It never occurred to Sam that Brookins would not be admitted at the Embers. "Once things get moving again, it'll be hopping around here. I gots to be ready. I'll be right here all night. Don't know when I'll go home. I have a cot in the storeroom. Got a radio. There's an easy chair and a lamp to read by. Got toilet articles, too. I stay here a lot."

"You mean you live here?"

"Sorta. I have a house. Small, but nice. Don't go there much. Ain't nobody there but me. There's always people here at the station. And there's always sompin to do. Helps fight the loneliness."

Sam didn't know quite how to respond. He just simply said, "I understand." He knew about loneliness.

Sam walked the three blocks to the Embers Restaurant. He really didn't walk. It was more of a step with his left leg and drag his right leg. The Chicago wind was living up to its reputation. He had no overcoat, just his uniform coat. He was about frozen when he got there. Brookins was right. It was a very nice, up-scale place. He slowly descended the flight of steps, one step at a time, being careful not to slip. Remembering his grandmother's instructions, he made sure everything was aligned and in its proper place before he opened the big oak door. Through the cut glass panels he could see several people waiting to be seated. *Might as well wait here, since I have nowhere else to go,* he thought to himself. *It'll be a nice change from the train station. I do wish Brookins had come with me.*

"Good evening, Captain Kennedy. Will there be one for dinner this evening, sir?" The maître d` was good. He had already surveyed Sam's name tag and rank before he approached the maître d`s stand.

"Yes, I'll be dining alone."

"I'll seat you now." And before Sam could say anything he was escorted to a corner table that overlooked Michigan Avenue and the lake. As he carefully made his way to the table, men shook his hand and women reached to touch his arm. No one seemed upset that he walked in off the street and was seated without waiting. Everyone smiled as he walked by.

The table was covered with a fine linen tablecloth and set with fine china, silver, and crystal. He couldn't figure out what all the extra forks and spoons were for though. He was an Oklahoma farm boy. He wasn't used to this. The menu had things on it he had never seen, things he couldn't pronounce. And it was expensive. *Boy, I'm sure a long way from the farm. If only Jessie could be here,* he thought to himself. And he missed her more.

He noticed that as people finished their dinner they would all come by his table to shake his hand. Or say welcome home. Or wish him a merry Christmas. He wasn't sure why. Maybe it was because he was the only person in uniform. Or because it was Christmas Eve. Or maybe it was the medal around his neck. That thing had gotten him more attention than he liked.

About half way through his steak, he sat straight back in his chair. He suddenly remembered that he had given the shoeshine boy a large tip. *"Oh no. I'll bet I don't have enough to pay for dinner. I'll get to spend Christmas either in jail or washing dishes."* Neither of which sounded very appealing but wouldn't surprise him. He finished his dinner as best he could. The waiter kept filling his water glass and coffee cup. It was nice to have coffee that wasn't like black molasses. He was convinced that some of the stuff the army called coffee really came out of tank transmissions.

He sat there enjoying the atmosphere long enough. It was time to confess his freeloading. He motioned for the Maître d`.

"Yes, Captain Kennedy, how may I assist you?"

"I need to discuss my check. It seems I've ma..."

Before Sam could confess his sin, the maître d' interrupted, "You have no check, sir. Do you see the couple at the table by the piano? That's the Bellamy's. They are paying for your dinner."

"They don't know me. Why would they do that?" Sam was relieved to know, regardless of the reason that he wouldn't have to add dishpan hands to his list of battle scars.

"Our policy is that no person in uniform has to pay for his meal. All of our patrons know this and are happy to do it. We will continue this policy until the war is over. Please accept your dinner with Mr. and Mrs. Bellamy's compliments."

Sam didn't know quite what to say or do. He had noticed that the Bellamy's had periodically looked his way. Now he knew why. At that moment, both of the Bellamy's approached his table. They expressed their gratitude for his service to the country. They were honored to have had him as their guest for dinner. They inquired about home and family and other pleasantries. He explained he was snowbound. He said he missed Jessie. They asked him to join them for dessert, to which he graciously declined. He thanked them for their generosity. They held his hands warmly as they wished him a quick trip home. They said good bye and returned to their table. He was overwhelmed by their warmth and kindness to a perfect stranger.

He stood, straightened his uniform, and placed his hat under his left arm so his right one would be free to assist him up the steps. He made sure that the blue ribbons and the gold eagle were perfectly placed. Then he began to make his way to the door. And as he did, everyone in the restaurant stood and clapped. And just as before, they touched his sleeve and shook his hand and thanked him as he passed by.

He had only taken a few steps when he stopped dead in his tracks. He was frozen, staring straight at the entrance. There standing by the Maître d` was an angel. Jessie. Sensing something was wrong, the clapping ceased as suddenly as it began. Everyone remained standing and stared at Sam. Like Moses parting the Red Sea, the Maître d` waved his arms and those standing between them made a pathway. They had not seen each other for over three years. She had not seen how badly he limped. Or the scar across the back of his left hand. Or the one over his left eyebrow. Jessie ran to him. Jumped in his arms. Kissed his scar. Wiped away his tear. And said, "Samuel Kennedy I love you!"

His tears were flowing. All Sam could do was hold her as tightly to him as possible, afraid that if he let go all that he was would pour out on the floor in a puddle around her feet. "Jessica Montgomery, will you marry me?"

"Yes! Yes! Yes!"

The applause thundered. Cheers rang out into the street as they stood and held each other alternately crying and laughing.

"How'd you get here?"

"Mr. Brookins brought me. He's standing right outside." They both turned to see. But he wasn't there.

"How'd you get to Chicago?"

"It's a very strange story. I'll tell you later. When I got to the station and couldn't find you, I just sat down on the bench in front of the platform doors and sobbed.

"Then the voice of an angel spoke my name, 'Miss Jessie, I know where Cap'n Sam is. I'll take you there.' I looked up and all I saw at first was this giant smile with a gold tooth."

"Miss Jessie, I'm Brookins. I's been watchin' out for your young soldier. You feel like walking a short distance? Come on, I'll take you to him. All he done for two days is talk 'bout you. You're a lucky girl. I know you ain't seen him in a long time. He has trouble walkin' good. So you be real gentle with him."

"Then he takes my hand. Pulls me up. And off we go. It was like magic. I don't remember getting here. It was like he snapped his fingers and there you were. I asked him to come in, but he wouldn't. He said he'd see us later."

They stood hugging and kissing for what seemed like hours. And all the while everyone in the restaurant kept standing and clapping.

The Maître d' shook Sam's hand, opened the door, and said, "Thank you Captain Kennedy for being our guest on Christmas Eve. And thank you, Miss, for giving us all a special gift. Please have a safe journey. Merry Christmas. God bless you."

Sam managed a Merry Christmas and thank you. Jessie took him by the arm to help him up the steps. But mostly just to touch him. As they walked back to Union Station, the applause still rang in him ears. The words of the Maître d' and the Bellamy's rolled over and over in his mind. He went there alone and empty. He left filled to overflowing.

No cars were on the snow-covered streets. The sky was so clear that it was more blue than black. Like millions of Christmas tree lights, the stars acknowledged those below as they blinked their approval from their celestial watch posts. And at that moment Sam thought to himself *miracles happen in the strangest places and at the most unexpected times.*

Union Station was virtually deserted, except those who had to be there to help others get to where they were going. Like Leroy Brookins. He hadn't seen him since their return from dinner.

They sat in Sam's familiar spot, the bench in front of the main doors to the tracks. Jessie sat as close to him as she could, almost in his lap. She slid both of her arms around his, then laid her head on his shoulder, and smiled. Sam stared at the sign above the door, "Home." "I know it's not Duncan, but this sure feels like home," Sam whispered to Jessie.

"I know," she said. "I know." And they both drifted off to sleep.

"Cap'n. Miss Jessie. Ya'll better wake up now. Your train'll be leaving soon. I done loaded your baggage. Everything's been took care of. I saw to it personally. You gonna be home on Christmas after all."

When Brookins spoke it was with uncommon clarity. His voice commanded attention. But it was always soothing and comforting. It was like the voice of a wise, old grandfather.

They both sat up. Moved their heads and necks to get out the kinks. Jessie stood. Straightened her clothes. Then reached down to help Sam. Brookins looked just like he did the first time Sam saw him.

"Mr. Brookins, I can't thank you enough for watching over Sam for me. And for taking me to him last night." Jessie was sweetly. "You will always have a special place in my heart." Then she put her arms around him as far as she could and hugged him tight.

Sam wasn't good with words. "Brookins, I will never forget you."

At that moment, spontaneously, Sam reached around

him neck. Unhooked the blue cloth ribbons. Then he placed his medal around Brookins' neck. "I want you to have this."

Brookins just stood there. Eyes filled with tears. Speechless. He reached in the side pocket of his overalls and pulled out a rectangular box about six inches long and four inches wide. It was wrapped in bright red paper.

"Cap'n Sam, you wuz nicer to me than anyone has been in a long time. I wants you to have this. Don't know anybody else has 'nough love to give it to. But you can't open it 'till the train is outa the station." Then he put it in Sam's hand and bear-hugged him.

"Board." The conductor's voice signaled it was time to go.

Brookins put one arm around each of them. "You kids get goin' now." Jessie kissed him on the cheek. Sam shook his hand. And then they boarded the train.

Sam was both anxious and excited about opening Brookins' gift. He unwrapped one corner and slid the red paper off. It was a black, hinged box. One he had seen many times. He opened it from the bottom. There was a gold eagle holding a gold star inside a wreath, and all attached to two blue strips of cloth. It had a piece of paper underneath read: Jessie took the paper and read it as Sam held the box.

"For conspicuous valor while in the face of imminent danger, without regard for personal safety... this Medal of Honor is awarded posthumously to Leroy L. Brookins."

Sam's hands were shaking. Jessie reached over, took the box from him and put her hand on his. "Isn't this just like the one you gave Mr. Brookins?" Sam just nodded yes. Jessie took the medal out of the box and clasped it around Sam's neck.

They rode in silence for a while. Sam holding the box and

citation. Jessie holding Sam's hands, gently rubbing the scar.

"Sammy, this whole time I've felt like someone was watching over me and guiding me to you. Like a guardian angel. And when I say you, I knew it."

"And he lives in Union Station."

A Place to Go on Christmas Eve

This collection of stories was designed and typeset by Sandra Van Winkle using Adobe InDesign.

Typography is Book Antiqua 12 point for body text. Chapter headers are Gabriola.

Gabriola is a display typeface designed by John Hudson. Named after Gabriola Island, in British Columbia, Canada. The Gabriola font can add elegance and grace to titles, subheads and other situations in which a more decorative style of type is appropriate. (http://www.microsoft.com/typography/fonts/family.aspx?FID=372)

Glyph and cover design was created in Adobe Illustrator.

Steven Roberts

A Place to Go on Christmas Eve

CPSIA information can be obtained
at www.ICGtesting.com
Printed in the USA
LVOW08s1018221217
559940LV00003B/10/P